Bright

White

ISBN 978-1-62880-256-6

First edition, April 2013

Printed in the United States of America on acid free paper

Published by Westview, Inc.
P.O. Box 605
Kingston Springs, Tennessee 37082
www.publishedbywestview.com

Bright

White

What really happened in

Sun Valley

By Carl Massaro

iv

Introduction

This is just a campfire yarn, a tall tale. None of this really happened like this, I just made it up. The village of Triumph is an odd little town. It was once a company town and from 1889 to 1959 it had hundreds of little cabins scattered around that miners threw together. The investors behind the company were big East Coast Philadelphia money and the minerals that the mountain contained were what the US currency was based on: gold, silver, copper, lead, and zinc. The gold in the Triumph is bonded to pyrite and when it oxidizes it becomes acidic. So it's not like California gold or Yukon gold. It's stubborn and problematic.

In 1963, the Triumph Mining Company sold the town, with restrictions, to a Lutheran Church group from North Dakota. The utopia they envisioned failed because they were just human and man is such a crazy animal. I'll save that tall tale for another book. This is the story of men who are gone, a story in between the horse and the turbocharger, a small part of the giant machine that ran nonstop, full-throttle, right into World War II.

I dedicate this book to my pop, who fought in that war and spent the rest of his life reading books in an effort to understand it. I dedicate this to my good buddy, mentor and stepfather, Rupper House, who wore his back out in this mountain and loved it. And I thank Jack Rutter for the lessons and stories he shared with me and that good coffee. Also a special thanks to Averell Harriman for two things: Harriman State Park, where as a boy I grew to love the outdoors, and the Sun Valley ski area. I have traveled the world skiing and there is no place like it. DON'T TELL ANYBODY.

Sincerely,
Carl Massaro

Chapter One

It was the fall of 1973; there was a gas shortage. I just put $500.00 down on a brand new Chevy Blazer 4x4, blue and white, V-8. I was going west. But first I had to see my friend, Jimmy Warner in Stowe, Vermont. We went to the ski patrol shed. Hale Wilhelm was the head of the ski patrol and an ex-10th Mountain Division Ski Trooper. He said he would write us a letter of introduction to Paul Ramlow, the head of the ski school at Sun Valley, Idaho, who had also been in the 10th Mountain Division. That's where I was going. Not sure why, just going. So I bolted a 40-gallon tank in the back of the Chevy, and piped it to the gas tank, pulled onto I-80 West and crossed the Delaware. Four days later, and a lot of gas, I pulled into Ketchum, Idaho.

Chapter Two

Two weeks later, I had my ski school jacket and a room in the attic of the Sun Valley Inn. I was settled in, so I went to town to have a beer. Right in the center of Main Street was a big, black, 1956 Cadillac limo parked in front of a joint called The Alpine Bar and Grill.

I walked into a log room with a giant mural of the olden days on the wall behind the bar. At the end of the bar was this old, white-haired woman in a '40s style cocktail dress. She sat nursing a drink and smoking a cigarette in one of those smoking things, ya know, like a holder. She looked like something out of an old black and white movie.

I sat down a couple of seats from her and ordered a beer. I'm not saying nothing. I'm minding my own.

In walks this girl, big girl, tall. She sits down in between me and the woman.

"Gin and tonic," she says. She puts her books on the bar, they look like schoolbooks: chemistry, history.

The bartender barks, "Margaux, you're only seventeen."

And, "Okay, okay," she says. "I'm eighteen. Just give me club soda. I'm gonna be nineteen next week."

So he does, turning his back grumbling something about her not being twenty-one and he didn't need to get a fine. As soon as he turns, she pulls a flask and pours.

"Margaux," I said, "what kind of name is that?"

"It's my name. What's yours?"

"Carl."

"Well, I'll call you Carlo," and she rolls the "r" with a continental flair.

Then the old woman opens up her mouth and out comes this voice that sounded like a Hudson River tugboat captain. "Carlo, Margaux -- what's this, a Dago joint? I feel like I'm in South Philly. You're a little young to be drinking at four thirty, kid."

"What's it to ya?" Margaux replies, with a lot of chutzpah for a school girl.

"I own this joint. My name's Posey, like the flower that I am, or was… Is that the new ski school outfit, *Carlo*?" She rolls the "r" too.

What gives with this place, I thought.

"That's the most god-awful color. Orange, looks like a prison uniform." Posey was hardly a flower.

"I don't pick the colors. I'm new on the line up."

"I remember when the ski school had nice colors." She took a drag, took a sip then turned her gaze to Margaux. "You like chemistry?" she said, pushing her glass towards the books on the bar.

"I hate chemistry," said Margaux. "I'm dropping out of school and I'm going to ski all winter with my private instructor, Carlo." She nudged me.

"I hate chemistry too," said Posey. "My husband was a chemist. He made me rich, then he died. We lived in New Jersey, like you."

"How'd you know I'm from Jersey?" I said.

"How'd you know?" she said, exaggerating a thick Nicky Newark accent. "We lived in Cherry Hill. He, my husband, worked for DuPont. Came out here in 1934 to hunt birds. I never went back. Things were different then. Those were the days."

Margaux offered her hand. "Hi, I'm Margi Hemingway. Pleased to meet you."

Posey waved her cigarette around. "I know who you are. I knew your grandfather." She looked up at the painting. "Yep," she sipped her glass, "Those were the days."

Chapter Three

In the early 1920s, DuPont and General Motors were partners. They embarked on the grand scheme of the American auto. John D. Rockefeller was in control of the oil fields and crushed his competition wherever possible. Many Americans forget that Henry Ford's first car was designed to run on alcohol distilled back on the farm. Gasoline caused severe engine knocking, so DuPont chemists searched for an additive that would increase the power of the fuel and stop the knocking. After a few years of dangerous experiments, they came up with a devil's brew: Tetraethylene lead, TEL, a concoction so dangerous that it killed several hundred factory workers in the most horrible and contorted ways. They went mad, saw demons and winged creatures, and heard voices. They had uncontrollable intestinal cramping and lost body functions. Close to a hundred were locked up, strapped down to steel beds, and closed off from the newspapers in "The House of Butterflies," near Penns Grove, New Jersey. They lay in their own shit for weeks as they slowly died. Posey's husband was a young chemist for DuPont and was exposed to small amounts of this material in the lab.

In December of 1930, Posey lay on the bed of her Cherry Hill home, exhausted and slightly bruised. Her husband had just finished a volley of violent sex and was down in the kitchen screaming, "Milk! I want milk. God damn it, where's the milk…"

He had been getting worse, with violent, crazy, headaches. He heard voices. She was becoming afraid of him. This was not the man she married.

Posey was a very beautiful woman and she and Ted had always had a powerful love for each other, but this was different. In the morning, he would not remember a thing.

She awoke and went down to the kitchen of her comfortable, suburban home. Ted was having his coffee and reading the morning paper,

"How are you darling?" she said.

He didn't lift his head out of *The Philadelphia Daily Record.* "More bank closings. People are lined up out front of Bankers Trust on Walnut Street. One woman fainted. People are losing their life's savings."

"I know, dear. It's awful." She petted his head like a puppy. "How are things at the lab, dear?" She knew something was wrong.

"It's killing me," he barked. "I don't want to talk about it."

Ted Gruner was about to make a breakthrough that would change his life. He was working on a process to stabilize gunpowder. Working with the chemicals Dinitrotoluene (DNT) and Trinitrotoluene (TNT), these were going to kill him, but they made him wealthy. No one said it would be easy. He had invested his earnings into stocks and back before insider information was illegal, he made a small fortune.

The Tetraethylene lead he worked on for gasoline was now in great demand. It was the age of the airplane and gasoline needed lots of octane to operate at 10,000 feet, where the air was thin. DuPont held all those patents and IG Farben was paying handsome royalties for the use of those formulations.

While the people were standing in line to get their money out of the failed banks in Philly, Ted and Posey were members of the Cherry Hill Country Club, going to horse races, and buying fine clothes at John Wanamaker's. But he was paying a high price, they both were -- the chemicals he worked with, the triethylene chlorides, and their cousins, would be used in later years by "ravers" to enhance sexual pleasure and create a warm fuzzy feeling. But now, when workers were exposed to high concentrations, they died, and Ted would soon die of liver failure from prolonged lab exposure. In the mean time, he was one horny guy.

The creation of triple-base propellants allowed big ship guns to deliver a projectile miles away. The gangsters in South Philly had more scruples than all these guys back in 1935. The Mob just wanted to bet on the ponies and make a little brew, maybe rule South Philly. These college boys didn't care what country they crushed on the way to the party.

Chapter Four

Rupert held on to his skis as the North Star tram car came around the bullwheel. He jumped into the car that had just dumped its load of ore into the hopper of the mill. Many of his buddies did the same thing every day. After their shift in the tunnels, they would ski down the hill from the Plummer tunnel to the village of Triumph. If the store was still open, Rupert would have a coke before he went home.

The progress in the Plummer tunnel was going well. They were working on widening the tunnel that ran through the Baby Ethel claim and came out in the American Eagle at the Triumph Shaft. He was the boss down here, men showed him respect in this hole.

When he came out the other side of the hill, the Idaho moon was in all its glory. God, it was so bright after being in the ground. A few short steps and he was to the elevator that took him down 800 feet to the lower workings.

Here they hoped to find another big face of galena like the one that was discovered in the Plummer tunnel. It was one for the record books, 700 feet long, 50 feet tall, 1,000 feet straight into the mountain.

A couple of billion years ago, this rock was exposed to hot boiling magma that got stirred up by the great Yellowstone Caldera. The lava turned the galena family metals--silver, gold, and zinc--to a gaseous flow that forced its way through the cracked rocks and cooled, leaving the veins that became the lifeblood of the Triumph Mine.

The mill and the Ketchum smelter were built by the Philadelphia Mining and Smelting Company, run by a Swiss Jew named Meyer Guggenheim. Meyer started out selling silver and stove polish door to door, but after years of consolidation, his American Smelting and Refining Company had the largest stake in the Hearst mining empire. The Hearst mines were going to be sold by the son of that hard-working miner. Like many times in history, the son gets spoiled rotten and pisses away daddy's fortune.

None of that mattered to Rupe, he had no stock, he was a miner, and on a cold, clear Idaho night, with the air outside at minus 20, it was warm and damp down at 700-foot level.

"How are the pumps running, Rowdey?" asked Rupe.

"Okay, boss, number one and number five are running full-bore and the rest are just kicking on once in awhile. Did ya' bring your boards up tonight?" Rowdey cut a big smile at his boss.

The two had gotten pretty good at flying off the hill at the end of the shift. This was the night shift, so they would get to come of the hill at seven in the morning. Right after the blast, the snow would be settled, hell, the whole mountain would be settled after the blast.

The Triumph had close to 90 miles of tunnel and thirty crews working in teams to drill and blast a continuing maze, like an ant farm.

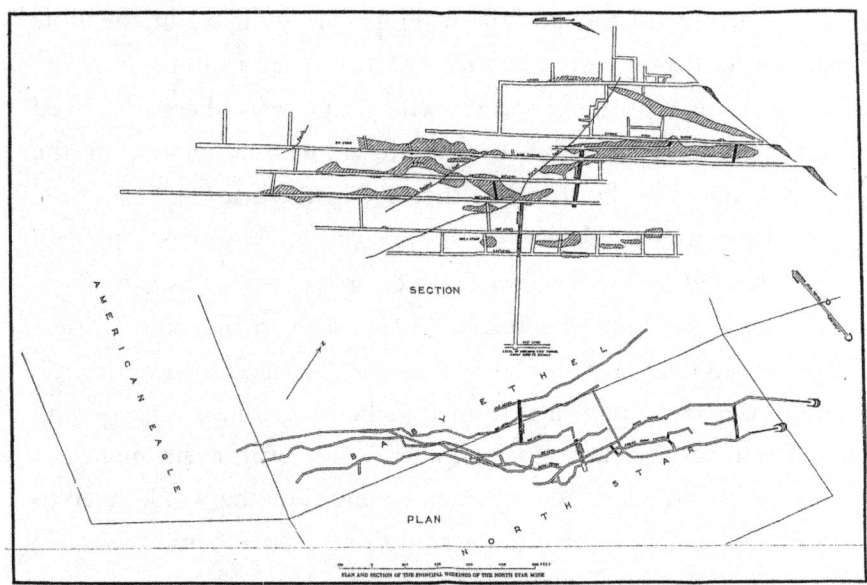

Figure 23. Plan and section of the principal workings of the North Star Mine (Plate 24 *in* U.S. Geological Survey Bulletin 814).

Each crew would arrive at their assigned location and clean up the blast from the preceding shift, set pre-cut timbers and blocking to hold the tunnel together, then drill holes in the tunnel in a prescribed pattern that would blow an 8x8x6 block out of the tunnel.

All the crews in the hill would set their powder to go at about the same time at the end of the shift. They would leave a twenty-minute fuse lit and head for the surface.

One time, after a huge three-day snow fall, the earth rumbled after the blast and brought down an avalanche that killed a lot of men.

The operation took years to recover. But by 1938, not only had it recovered, it was cooking. Pay was good. Folks back in the cities were suffering with the Great Depression, people were going hungry, but in the Triumph, you got paid eight or ten bucks for a hard day's work.

Miners rode the bus up from Hailey or lived in the little village that was an eclectic mix of blacks and chinnies in the bunk house, a preacher and his wife, and a few others who lived in the little shacks in the company town, who cut wood, ran the post office and school at the other end of the place.

When the six o'clock whistle blew, Rupert started up from the lower levels, checking on his men as he coaxed them out.

"Let's go, boys. Daybreak. Coffee's on in the bunkhouse." He looked up at a dozen men working the big face of silver ore. Some were tying the final fuses together and others were getting the air tools and hoses secured. Up the elevator, six men at a time, it would take a few minutes up and then, he would have to head back through the mountain in the Plummer tunnel to come out at the North Star gravity tram.

When he exited the tunnel, his skis were set up alongside the privy. He was strapping them on when Rowdey came out and followed suit.

"What a day. Ah, you can't have better weather that this for skiing." Rowdey pushed off.

The big boards sliced through the few inches of new powder that had fallen on the hard-packed snow underneath. The grassy hills had been burnt by fires set by the company last spring as ground-control measures. It made for a pretty good terrain.

Down they went, like a couple of pros. They had done this a lot of times before. Behind them, several other miners were setting out, following their lead.

As the sun came up December 1 of 1938, seven men descended the North Star bowl, howling like wild Indians as America's first real destination ski resort was making ready for its big debut, right on the other side of the mountain.

Chapter Five

Averell Harriman had spared no expense. He had made a fortune in the railroad and mining businesses. Brown Brothers and Harriman had joined forces and created the largest brokerage house on Wall Street. Now they were going to party at a whole other level. Harriman built a 5 star resort on the St. Moritz model, used his railroad to run his customers and clients right in from New York and Hollywood. He had hired one of New York's most prestigious advertising firms to unveil Sun Valley to his world of wealthy American industrial families. There was a list of several hundred guests invited, all expenses paid, to the biggest ski party ever held.

Numerous Broadway stars and many of Wall Street's available men were paying their way to be part of the opening celebration. It was part real estate promotion and part political maneuvering. The drums of war were beating in Europe and Brown Brothers Harriman were representing the resources of most of the biggest players from both sides.

Averell had enlisted Austrian Count Felix Schaffgotsch to find the best place in the West and this was it--high desert, very dry, very sunny, cold, clear nights where the stars practically jumped in your lap.

Harriman hired a young newspaper reporter named Ernest Hemingway to write some PR articles. Hemingway quickly fell in love with the Rocky Mountain characters that were there for the mining and cattle operations, the smelters, railroad yards, logging operations and the millions of sheep. They called them Mountain maggots, It was the real deal, the American West, and now on a Saturday night at the Alpine Bar, you're going to find miners, cowboys and them "East Coast people."

The stage was set for a very happy new year.

Chapter Six

Rowdey was having a cold beer and shooting a game of 8 ball. His game was fair for a kid who grew up in Hailey, Idaho. He didn't gamble, he was just there for a little fun. It had been a hard week at the Triumph. He was there with some of the boys: Jack Rutter, the Surface Boss, Willard Rember, head of the pipe fitting operation, and several of the hard rock miners.

There were not a lot of women in Ketchum in 1938. There were a few, at the bank, the County Courthouse, the Hot Springs Brothel, and school teachers. But mostly, Idaho in the winter was a man's world. So when the Sun Valley Company advertised for over a hundred young women to work in the hotel operations, restaurants and clothing shops --and they advertised in several of Averell's good buddy Randolph Hearst's papers in New York, San Francisco and Boston --well hell, that was stocking your favorite fishing stream with trophy trout.

Many of America's adventurous young women were ready to jump at the chance to spend a winter at a ski resort. Most of them were college-educated, upper-middle-class kids. They came out of the woodwork. Many of the local Idaho mountain boys couldn't believe their luck. As the girls walked in the door, the whole place changed: Nine girls, all pretty, all new in town for the winter. The boys stood up a little taller.

Rutter shuffled some coats that were on the bar stool and boldly said, "Ladies, welcome to the Alpine, center of the Idaho west. I'm Jack Rutter, at your service." He tipped his hat.

Jack was from the County Hertfordshire, near London. He was full of the confidence an education in engineering and architecture instilled in a man. He was the Surface Boss and overseer of the cable trams, timber mills, pump houses, and fabrication shops. He always wore a tie and heavy wool jacket. The English accent threw the gals for a loop.

Rowdey looked like he was kicked by a bull. This place, his watering hole that normally was full of crusty, old gamblers and has-been miners, was suddenly abuzz with the sound of women--not one or two--but almost a dozen. And one stood out to him above all the rest. She was tall and thin, with the shiniest skin he had ever seen. She had light brown hair and was very neatly dressed in jeans and a heavy sweater with what looked like snowflakes woven into the stitching. She wore a leather belt that matched her shiny English riding boots.

Rowdey, overtaken with a sudden super power, walked right up to her before she could even settle in the place. "I need a partner for mixed doubles, ma'am."

He was completely winging it, but Rup on the other side of the table picked up his lead in a hurry and gave a pool cue to a young gal seated at the bar. She too smiled and took hold of the stick.

"Oh, no thank you. My mother warned me about pool halls," said the young woman, as Rowdey's wall of confidence took a hit. "I'm not very good at billiards," she said.

"This is not billiards, ma'am." He was not taking 'no' for an answer. "This is 8 ball. Pay-table rules. I'll help ya' through it. My name is Rowdey McDonald."

He stretched out his hand and she reluctantly shook it.

"My name is Anna Thatcher. Is there a talc stone? I will need all the help I can get."

She quickly found the stone on the back wall and rubbed her hands. Then with the grace of a St. Louis parlor shark, she ran in four balls.

"There, that's a good start. Your turn, cowboy." She looked at Rupert and gave him a little wink.

This was shaping up to be a pretty good Saturday night. So far. Rupert suddenly looked a little worried he was about to get an ass whipping in 8 ball.

As the evening progressed, the two couples, or teams, had four drinks, some really good laughs and realized that they all loved adventure, challenge, and winter. The winter was clean and new, like tomorrow.

Chapter Seven

It was a quick walk for Averell Harriman from The Union Bank on Broadway to Street to 1 Wall Street. He had a good breakfast served at the top of his skyscraper by his personal chef. He felt light as sea foam thinking about his new ski area. He was getting daily reports from his project managers. His magazine interests, through Hearst's Time Magazine, were talking up the million dollar price tag--a big number in a depression, but fact is, it was peanuts for him. He owned lots of stock in the major manufacturers of all the products going into the development.

He called his baby brother, Bunny. "Bunny, we need 2 miles of our best cable for our new chair lift device, and some bullwheels."

"Okay, Averell. I'll call our friends at Thyssen Steel." Bunny was always ready to please his older brother.

They all had made a great deal of money on the German military buildup. The Thyssen steel works and the Anglo-German Friendship Society were two sides of the same wooden nickel. With friends like that, who needs enemies.

"The bullwheels and cable should be in stock, sir, at our Bethlehem plant." Bunny announced.

Every major mine in America had a bullwheel atop the headframe that pulled up the elevators. Bethlehem made them in several sizes.

Averell put his feet up on his shiny walnut desk. "I want the cable woven two miles long in one piece, Bunny," said Averell. "I want the bullwheels primed and fitted for extra heavy use. I also need 60 tons of 4 inch by 1/2 high-nickel steel angle-iron and two tons of 7/8's bridge rivets. Carla will send you over the list. Oh, and make sure you get it loaded in Pittsburgh on our Express Freight to Ogden with priority."

"Will do." Bunny tightened up at the thought of Carla. Averell's secretary was a looker. "Will she be bringing that list over herself?" He was hopeful.

"In your dreams," Averell returned, expecting it. "And make sure the cable is on the biggest spool they have. Call me when it's loaded in the yard."

This was Averell's number one project. The steel and rail businesses were beginning to expand, so were fuel and mineral production. He was on the phone with the Bureau of Mines in Pittsburgh at least once a week regarding funding of mineral, oil and gas developments. One of which was the Triumph Mine in Sun Valley. When Averell hunted, he always killed two birds with one stone.

Chapter Eight

The Brighton Rope Works in Wilkes-Barre, Pennsylvania had a giant machine called a planetary strander. It looked much like the lace manufacturing equipment that Meyer Guggenheim pioneered for weaving in Hoboken, New Jersey, but instead of Irish lace, the machine wove bundles of seven strands of high-carbon steel wire into clusters, then took seven of those clusters and ran them through giant tensioning rollers and twisted the metal. This process gave it a memory, so it wanted to stay that way. There were forty-nine huge spools, eight feet tall, set on a long track in a building big enough to park a battleship in. These wires ran the gantlet and were whipped into shape--the shape being a 1 ¼-inch cable, two miles long on one big spool, as in *BIG*.

Harriman was instrumental in organizing the National Recovery Review Board for Roosevelt. The steel mills in Scranton and Wilkes-Barre were all under the control of Bethlehem Steel, a Brown Brothers Harriman asset. When the phone rang at the Wilkes-Barre plant head office, Mr. Willcott's secretary quickly put the call through.

"Hello," Willcott wondered what this was about. "How are things in New York today?"

"Fine," said Bunny, "very well, thank you. Mr. Willcott, we are building a ski resort at one of our western rail stops in Ketchum, Idaho and we are designing a tram machine to lift skiers up the mountain in chairs. This is a new concept and we want the best cable you can make us. It needs to be two miles long in one piece. And we need it as soon as possible."

"Well…" Mr. Willcott stood up at his desk and looked out over a very quite factory floor. The Depression was killing the steel-wire business and there was considerable worker unrest from union organizers. "Two miles will take some doing, but we could have it done in two or three weeks." He was singing Bunny's song.

"Great, I'll take two like that," said Bunny. "We will wire you a formal order this afternoon and we will set up a flat car through our U-P and Pennsylvania Railroad affiliates." Bunny loved the power he had over these factory bosses. "Oh and Mr. Willcott, we won't forget this. Thank you. Good bye."

He hung up the phone and felt relived, time for lunch. He was meeting a young woman who worked at the 39 Broadway office. Her name was Marjory Goodspeed.

Margie was working at the banking division of the Union Banking Corporation. She was seventeen, but lied about her age. She came to New York to find fame on Broadway. Bunny was crazy about her. She was just a teller and was well aware that he was her superior, but she was a modern woman on the move in Manhattan.

Margie ran away from Buhl, Idaho when she turned fifteen and like many young women, rode the Greyhound east, seeking fame and fortune in the "Big Apple". She was very lucky to find a job at Union Banking.

Union was a Brown Brothers Harriman affiliate used for funneling monies back and forth between the Thyssen steel operations in Germany and the Pennsylvania steel companies.

Marg knew how to work a crowd and she was meeting Bunny for lunch at Katz's, and if things went well, Sardi's for drinks.

Chapter Nine

Ed Swent, the superintendent of the Triumph Mining Company, was meeting with Rutter at the compressor room. The noise was like being inside a giant squeeze box. He was able to take the phone line outside and close the insulated door.

"What do ya want?" barked the big Swede.

"Ed, this is Harold Knight down at the Ogden Yard. I'm involved in a project on Bald Mountain in Ketchum up there by you."

Harold had helped Ed with timely boxcar deliveries of powder and supplies and they went back awhile. Plus, they were both deacons in The Church of Latter-day Saints.

"I need some help, Ed. We got a spool of cable coming your way that's awfully heavy."

Harold's tone was inconsistent with his usual positive approach. When a man runs trains in the Rockies, there's not much he can't do.

"How heavy?" Ed had the field phone tight against his ear.

"It could be 110 ton with the spool and the spool will be 20 feet around and 16 feet across. It will hold two miles of 1 ¼ steel wire for that chairlift machine they are putting up on that hill. I got to get it from the rail yard at Ketchum to the bottom of the east side of Bald Mountain and I was thinking you got those two RD8's I delivered you last month, so you might give that spool a nudge."

24

Harold knew he was asking for a miracle. He waited a moment for the Swede's response.

"Nudge? At 110 ton, it's gonna take a pretty big nudge. When's it coming?"

"Swent would go to the moon if you asked nice. There was a kind of code among these guys, if it was within the length of their cable tow, they would pull ya. If not, they'd go get a longer cable.

"Should be a couple weeks. The big bosses want it to get extra treatment. This ski area is a number one priority for the company. If anything goes wrong, I'll get my walkin' papers." Harold sounded serious.

"I guess I could save your ass, bud. You bet, we'll strap two lowboys together with some I-beams and ease that little darlin' right where you want her. Should be worth couple of train tickets for the wife and I down to sunny California. She's got a sister down there that just had twins and she wants to see 'em." Ed knew Harold would give him a train pass anywhere anytime.

"Thanks, brother. I'll call you when it gets to Ogden." Harold sounded relived.

"Hey, Harold, why can't we just offload it right there. It's a straight shot from the tracks to where that lift is going. We bought some timber from Ivie Logging last week that came off that mountain right there." Ed saw the whole plan in his mind.

"That'll work, Ed. I'll have a yard crane tagged onto the flat car to lift it some. Between the Cats and that crane, we should be okay. Thanks." The call ended. The task was as good as done.

Chapter Ten

Bunny pushed open the Ludlow Street entrance to Katz's and Margie made her entrance. She expected the place to be full of show people wannabes and her entrance was very important. This was the world of "The Image." People knew that Bunny was a banker and Broadway was always looking to befriend a banker.

"You go freshen up, kiddo." Bunny looked over the room. "I'll go get our ticket." Everything at Katz's runs with a ticket.

"Hello, Mr. Harriman," said the young man at the counter.

"Hello. What's our special today?"

"Every-ting is special." The thick, Yiddish accent just flowed in this place.

Bunny and Margie would have lunch, be seen, and then grab a cab Uptown, to the Pennsylvania Hotel. There they would make love for a few hours in the suite that the company kept there. They have been carrying on like this for a month now.

Marg had the corned beef and orange soda. Bunny had the pastrami. He was in a hurry to get Uptown. She was cool and wanted to make sure everybody saw her.

She had auditioned for several shows. She did real good for *There's Wisdom In Women* and thought she would get a small part, but she wasn't called back. Then she got a big break, thanks to Bunny, in *The Body Beautiful*. The name says it all. But after four nights, it closed. The producer thought she could gain a few pounds, so she was working on it.

"Now that's a sandwich." Bunny made room for the plates. They were both hungry.

"That's Mack Gordon, the composer," said Margie. "I'd love to work in one of his shows."

"I'll talk to him. These shows are always looking for investors." Bunny could play the "gold digger" game with the best of them.

They finished lunch and hurried Uptown for Bunny's high point of the week. He loved spending this kind of time with her. She was as hot as a firecracker in the sack and about wore him out. By five, they were both exhausted. They had tried every position they could think of and they used a whole box of condoms.

Bunny had to be extra careful, his senior partner, Prescott Bush, was one of the founding members of The American Birth Control League and sat on the board. They used a scientific study to show that 40 percent of all rubbers leaked. Then they bought up control in a company that made rubbers and were selling over 30 million a year. Their motto was, "Only caring parents should conceive in love…" Or some shit like that.

How would it look if Bunny knocked up a underage employee? *The Post* would have a field day.

Margie took a shower and he stepped in for another go.

"Bunny, no," she said. "You've had enough. I've got to get ready for Sardi's."

She slipped out. He pretended to pout, but he was just bluffing, his train had left the station.

Chapter Eleven

December in New York was bitter cold. The wind came down from upstate and swept across the Hudson. The air was clean and Christmas decorations were getting dusted off in the back storage rooms of the big department stores. As Bunny and Margie walked up Seventh Avenue to Times Square, the lights of the giant Planters Peanut glistened. A light rain had fallen earlier and the whole world was washed. The marquees flashed "Dean Martin" and another boasted "Times Square Lady."

Marg had read about it in *The Post*, the story of a small town girl that inherits her rich uncle's bookie business and gets squeezed by the mob, only to be saved by a tough-guy songwriter. Jesus, she thought, who comes up with this shit--a tough-guy songwriter?

They arrived at Sardi's at exactly 7:15 p.m., along with a small crowd of show biz people. At 7:15 sharp, almost every day, Ira Katzenberg walks in and is greeted by Vincenso Sardi, who exercises the art of "The Fine Italian Hand," and places Ira at a table with a show man who wants to talk. Everyone wanted to talk with Ira Katzenberg, but today, it was Bunny's turn.

"So," Ira Katzenberg had a big smile that could swallow a shark. "Why is a banker coming to me today? Is the Depression over? And who is this lovely lady you brought with you?"

"Mr. Katzenberg," Bunny had prepared his spiel. "I represent a client that is developing a winter resort that is very new and we want to tell the story in film, with music. We feel this resort should reflect a wonderful, bright, promising future."

Ira lit up a cigar. "Okay, a story about the Catskills. I hope it's not a Christmas story." He smiled

"Not the Catskills. We are way out west, in Idaho. We are going to call it Sun Valley and we want to open with a bang."

"I think you should be talking to my friends in California. If you like, I can arrange a meeting."

"Well," Margie stepped up to the plate. "We want it to be a New York kind of show. Hi, I'm Marjory Goodspeed." She put out her perfect hand.

"Oh yes," said Bunny. "I'm sorry, this is Marjory. She works for our company."

"Well, your company has very good tastes." He figured her for a dancer when she walked in.

"I was thinking if we had a good song, ya know, everything starts with a song."

Bunny sat back and watched them work each other. He loved her passion, anything to do with show business. Every few minutes he would interject something like: "We want horses, and there will be a beautiful, big fireplace…"

But then Margie took the conversation over with her ideas about how the show might play, and how she would be perfect for a main part. For her, this would be a homecoming of extraordinary success. Buhl, Idaho was a little dust bowl, farm town, and she would show them all back there that she could make in the Big Apple.

After a half hour, Bunny stood up and went to the john, this would normally be Margie's signal to wrap it up, but she was sitting at Sardi's with the king of Broadway and this was a table she would have to be dragged away from.

This was a hand she had been playing for, for months. This was it, the proverbial big break, everybody dreams of one.

Bunny returned to the table and didn't sit down. "Well Marge. I'm sure Mr. Kaztenberg has other people to visit with and we have work tomorrow."

"Oh, no," said Ira. "I'm enjoying her fresh ideas, stay, stay, have another Manhattan." Ira stretched his arm out in a welcoming gesture.

"No, thank you, I really must be going. We have a big day tomorrow. Friday's payday and I have to get to the office very early." Bunny was beat, and if he had another drink he would probably fall asleep.

"Bunny, darling…" Marge dragged these words out of her sympathy vault, "would you mind if I stayed awhile? I'll catch a cab to my apartment. Please, dear?" She was cute enough to get anything she wanted. "Mr. Kaztenberg and I could talk about the movie, dear." She looked at Ira and he was fine with that.

"Sure thing, doll, but call me when you get home, okay?" Bunny halfway expected this. She was predictable and he did have a big day planned at the bank. On Fridays, money moved, lots of it, and money made the world go round.

Chapter Twelve

The Short Empire S-23 Flying Boat lumbered into the cold Atlantic currents of Port Washington, New York. It was carrying some very concerned gentlemen from the Rolls-Royce Aircraft Engine Division. They had arrived from London via Bermuda on the new transatlantic route. They were lucky to have made it. Little did they know, the cold Atlantic air was freezing up the fuel in the four, huge Bristol Perseus engines. Each was equipped with a special carburetor fuel heater, but when planes flew across the warm currents of the Gulf Stream, they were having trouble, and freezing up.

The four men arrived at the landing dock and quickly jumped into a waiting limousine for a ten o'clock meeting at 1 Wall Street. There would be several executives there from Ford Motors and DuPont.

The boardroom of Brown Brothers Harriman was a trophy to the American Empire: 50 feet long, with a huge walnut table that sat thirty people.

Averell, as always, sat at the head. Some of the men assembled were part of the Anglo-German Friendship Society. Several were also members of Skull and Bones.

Edsel Ford had opened the discussion, "Gentlemen, we at Ford Motors are ready, willing, and able to manufacture your engines provided you allow us to make some minor changes in the assembly that will be required for our production line."

He was lying. He knew his father wanted nothing to do with helping the English. Henry Ford's German plant was already producing war machines for the Third Reich and ole Henry had just personally authorized the printing of 500 copies of *The Protocols of the Elders of Zion*.

Sir Percival Perry was the Chairman of Ford in England. He was pushing for this deal. It was a very important deal. It meant life and death to his homeland.

The Merlin V-12 aircraft engine was the pride of the British Royal Air Force. But they couldn't build them fast enough. Germany's factories were turning out forty engines for every Merlin. They needed this deal, and Ford's US operations were feeling the grip of the Depression.

Sir Percival Perry brokered this meeting through his association with the Royal Air Academy. Henry Ford Sr. was not supportive, but he gave his son Edsel permission to meet.

They came to terms on the manufacture of the Rolls-Royce Merlin with all the patent rights and engineering remaining exclusively in Rolls-Royce's total control. With Ford's factories on Britain's side, the balance of power would level up a bit.

This was good business for DuPont because these planes used only very high octane TEL in the fuel. The gentlemen agreed on terms and conditions and Sir Perry returned the following day to London.

Two weeks later, Ford reneged on the deal and pulled out, leaving DuPont and Brown Brothers Harriman scrambling. They got Packard to do the deal with the help of DuPont's Pontiac tech support. The Pontiac boys respectfully made some changes to the bearing material and switched to a lead-zinc composite called indium. The bearings ran longer, smoother and the

engines built by the USA were soon sought after by the RAF
pilots. Zinc demand was moving up.

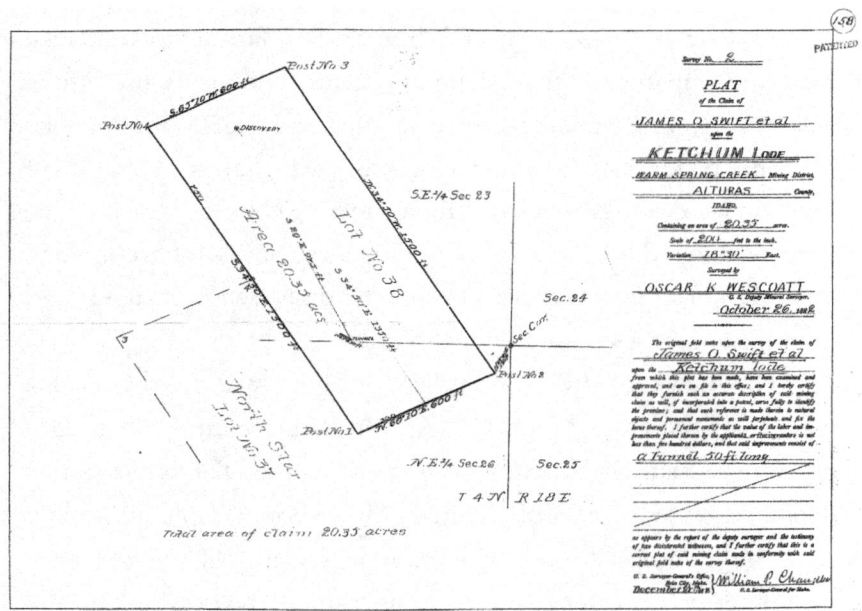

Chapter Thirteen

As Rowdey's crew worked "the Strike" farther to the west, into the unpatented federal mining claim known as the Annie Claim #54, "the Strike" grew even wider and the Triumph broke national production records. This was great, but the #2 and #3 pumps were working all the time now and the electrical usage was pushing the Idaho Power Company's limit. The company was up to 150 men now and if one couldn't keep up, Rupert had to replace him with someone who could.

The news of Adolph Hitler's exploits was in the Hailey paper. At the end of April 1937, Franco, in Spain, had brought in the German Air Force on his own people. There was a real feeling now that we would be in this war soon. People just knew.

The Triumph Mining Company was using all the timber it could get now from Galena Summit to the Maskot Mine, up the East Fork of the Big Wood River. Logs came in and Rutter's boys sawed them into timber sets. "The Strike" was as big as a football field now and six sets tall, so things in the hole were getting a little hairy.

"Damn," said Rowdey. "I'm beat and I can't wait for this week to be over. I'm gonna go up to Gruner's cabin for a midnight ski tour."

Posey had built a very remote cabin up Baker Creek near the hot springs. Skiers could walk up cleared logging trails or be pulled by a small Caterpiller tractor. The timber was conveniently cleared by logging to make ski runs. It was private, and only a select group knew about it. The cabin was very warm, more like a lodge, really. It was large and had a boiler in the basement that connected to a spring, so the building was very well-built with the same construction materials as the Sun Valley Lodge. The main hall was big enough for twenty people, with built-in window seats around a large stone and concrete fireplace.

Posey's driver, George, would be idling the little Cat at the entrance to the Baker Creek road. The snow was deep out there, maybe 10 feet, but the little Cat had a plowed a path that it would struggle all winter to keep in service.

George had a heated, canvas blanket that clipped around the engine cover of the machine that kept the engine heat blowing onto his legs. He wore a heavy fur coat that looked like something an Artic explorer would use, but it was December and the evening temps were in the 20's, maybe 15 at night.

He had his coat unbuttoned and a bottle of beer in his lap as he waited for the cars and pickups to roll up the highway from Ketchum.

Little wisps of steam were coming off some of the hillside hot springs as the late-evening sun lit up the Boulder Mountain range with a pink and purple sky.

This place was like heaven. Up here, you couldn't hear the madness building up in the old country. Up here, Basque expats and Austrian exiles could live in a new world, the American West, where sheep and cattle could live together with a minimum of friction and winter was a big time out, a time for fun, a time for people to let loose a little, sometimes a little too much.

Annie and some of her girlfriends were invited by a few of the Austrian ski instructors to come up for a party. She was looking forward to it. They had all heard about the remote cabin and were headed to the Alpine to board a bus that Posey arranged for the event.

Jack had asked Rowdey to take the company truck into the Chevy dealer in Ketchum for its service and they had ordered an optional PTO to be installed on the transmission to operate a rear wench. He brought it in about two and they said they could put it on right away. The new Chevy was a beaut: chrome bumpers, ton-and-a-half dually. The company had installed a steel bed and this PTO would operate a rear drum wench.

Rowdey went into the Alpine for a beer and thought he would just wait a few hours and pick up the truck and head out to Posey's for this party, but then she walked in.

Annie had not run into Rowdey for several weeks. He was working the night shift at the mine and she was on the desk at the hotel during the day.

She was perfect for the job, well-groomed, well-spoken, and well-educated. She studied biochemistry in college at Princeton, which was completely unacceptable for a young woman in 1936. Women were expected to learn shorthand and some business skills to serve in a corporate office under men, or in the nursing fields. It was still a man's world and the glass ceiling was nowhere in reach. Her father was a Princeton grad and laboratory scientist for Standard Oil of New Jersey. He died rather abruptly when she was just two.

"Hey, Annie." Rowdey didn't hesitate to show his enthusiasm. "Where have you been hiding?" She smiled and he thought she was happy to see him so he dove right in. "Have you been up on the hill skiing?" He thought she looked sunburned.

"Yes, I went on Monday afternoon. It was great. I get Mondays off. Maybe we could ski together next Monday."

She had made the second move. This was good.

"God, I wish I could," said Rowdey. "I'm on the night shift and it's getting a little dangerous down in the hole."

She saw an honest concern in his expression.

"I'm off tonight though."

He was always off Saturday and Sunday. He just came in for a few hours on Saturday to help Jack around the surface shops. Today he was dealing with the new truck.

"Why don't you come to our night-ski party at Baker Creek?" A voice from the table behind them had a thick German accent.

They both turned and saw a table full of Austrian ski school instructors.

"Where did you get that tan?" Rowdey fired the first shot and it was returned with a smile.

"We spend all day on the mountain. How about you, cowboy?" Audie was about the same age and build as the miner.

"I spend all day inside the mountain," he enjoyed the word play.

"Have a beer with us. I want that hat. Let me try that hat, cowboy." Audie reached, but Rowdey pulled back.

"Not for sale, fellas. I'll take a rain check on that beer."

"Okay, maybe next time."

There was no way he was going to let Annie near those wolves. "Hey, Annie, want to take a ride on the longest tram in the valley?" He took a shot.

"I thought I was riding the longest tram in the valley on Dollar Mountain," she seemed interested.

"You're riding the longest chairlift. My company runs three trams and one is over four miles long. Want to ride it? It runs all night." He was giving her his best pitch.

"Well, actually, some of my friends are going to go out to Baker Creek for this private party. There is a bus coming here in about twenty minutes. I'll tell you what, I'll keep an open mind about it, but not tonight." She didn't sound convincing.

"Come on, Annie. I'll be on my best behavior," he glanced at the table full of bright red jackets and suntanned men. "And I think you'll love it. Let me show you another Idaho." He was still hopeful.

How will I get home?"

"I'll get you back to the Inn, no problem." He knew the night watchman on the Independence would let him take his pickup to shuttle Annie over through the Elk Horn Ranch.

"You know," said Annie, "I think I trust you and I'm going to do it."

He was stunned by her blunt response.

"You're going to miss a great party," said Audie. "You should come with us."

Rowdey turned away from them, "Great. Okay. Where are your skis and boots?" He popped the question.

"Skis? You didn't say anything about skis. They're in my room." She was still in.

The two walked across the street and Rowdey signed the service receipt for the new truck. The service manager brought it around and left it idling.

The two jumped in. "Thanks for keeping her running, Donald." Rowdey tipped his hat and off they went up Sun Valley Road to the dorms at the Inn.

"Wanna come up?" She asked a loaded question.

"Sure," he said, and they bounded up the stairs past the rear kitchen doors.

The Inn was a busy place. About a dozen people were preparing food for several of the company operations. Annie lived in a small room above the kitchen with two bunk beds. The room was neat and tidy and the dorm had strict rules regarding visitors after hours. It was four thirty in the afternoon and there was still a lot of sunlight before that Idaho moon took the sky.

She grabbed her gear and turned around to see Rowdey in the doorway. To his surprise, she gave him a kiss on the cheek.

"Easy, cowboy," she read his mind. "The night's still young." And she bolted under his big arm and out the door. He followed like a ship in tow.

They drove down to the railhead just south of Ketchum where the Independence tram unloaded to a hopper that fed string rail cars.

The Independence Mill was the oldest on the mountain. It started in 1888 and ran intermittently, depending on demand.

Right now it was running because of government Orders for Minerals. The Bureau of Mines had set the price and quantity, as well as salaries and wages. It was like they were calling all the shots. Rowdey never gave much thought to any of this, especially tonight. He had one thing only on his mind tonight: Anna Thatcher, from Princeton, was going to sunset ski the backside of the Triumph with him. This is a big, damn deal, bud, he thought to himself.

They pulled the truck up in front of a large, timbered structure, half-barn, half-bin. There was a locked door with a standard company lock and Rowdey had a key. He opened the door that led to a wooden ramp with a platform and a cable moving around a bullwheel above several heavy wooden ore bins with two rail cars below the bins.

The bullwheel was just like the ski lift that Annie was used to, but instead of chairs, there were large steel bins, big enough to hold two people, if they were close. The cable was just $7/8^{th}$ diameter and the cars were about 400 feet apart.

As the bins came around the wheel, they were emptied by a trip lever and then reset by a cam before rounding the big wheel. As they came around, riders could jump in, but they needed to be quick about it.

The two stood on the platform for a few minutes and watched several cars come through.

"You'll need to get your skies in first and then hop in on the go. We get about five seconds and this tram won't stop, so keep your wits about ya." Rowdey was confident she could do this.

"This is like hopping a train," she said, as the next car clanked and relocked its lever.

"How would you know about hopping a train?" He laughed. "Ready?" He grabbed her hand. "Let's go," and as the car came around, they tossed in their gear and hopped in.

The big steel box swayed some as it passed over the first tower pulley. They were on their way, the late afternoon sun was falling behind the mountain and the blue Idaho sky was like an ocean.

The tram carried them across a frozen valley were elk wintered in large herds, the bulls perched on the hillsides like lookouts. A herd of about a hundred or so calmly grazed below them as they cabled across, just 30 feet above the ground.

They had traveled almost two miles when the car began to climb up the side of the Independence claims.

The Independence Mine was almost a separate operation, though connected by a small tunnel to the rest of the workings. The tunnels of the Independence were almost 1,000 feet above the Triumph Strike. There was a surface road, but in winter, most travel on the mountain was in it, through tunnels, or over it, with trams.

There were three trams in good working order in 1938. The North Star tram ran from the village of Triumph to the entrance to the Plummer tunnel, then you passed through the Plummer and came out at the elevator to "the Strike". There you could go down as much as 800 feet or you could pick up the tram that ran from the GE claim to the Little Giant on the Independence Mine works.

The work on this side of the mountain consisted of a small crusher, a stamp mill, a shaker table, and a tram building with ore bins that ran to the rail site about a half mile south of Ketchum, where Rowdey and Annie had jumped on.

As they approached the ore loading building on the hillside, Annie was all eyes and ears.

"Get ready," said Rowdey. "This one's a little bumpy."

The car rattled over the pulleys coming onto the site and Annie jumped out first, with Rowdey right behind her.

"Piece of cake." She didn't show any signs of fear.

It was a perfect December evening, the sky was still well-lit, though the sun was over the hill. The air was still and cool, there was plenty of snow on the hill.

Rowdey made arrangements with the mill supervisor to use his truck that was parked at the bottom of the hill. They would drive it across the elk feeding grounds the two miles to the rail head. The mill man would ride a car down the hill at the end of his shift. A simple lever could be thrown to prevent the ore car from being loaded. The mill man was happy to oblige.

They all liked the two perks they got with this job, and skiing was one of them. The other was men you could count on.

"Those are pretty nice skis, Annie." Rowdey was a little envious. He had seen the new metal-edged skis in one of the shops.

"Thanks," said Annie. "Two bucks a week on my ski shop account. We get a discount at the company store."

The Sun Valley Company gave accounts and encouraged all the employees to use the new equipment and ski well. They provided payment programs, ski lessons, and meals at employee prices that were very affordable.

Annie was a good skier and she took off first. Rowdey followed like a hound on the trail. They came down the first face of the Ida Harland claim and crossed in the Chicago. Then they stopped on a ridge overlooking a long, windblown saddle.

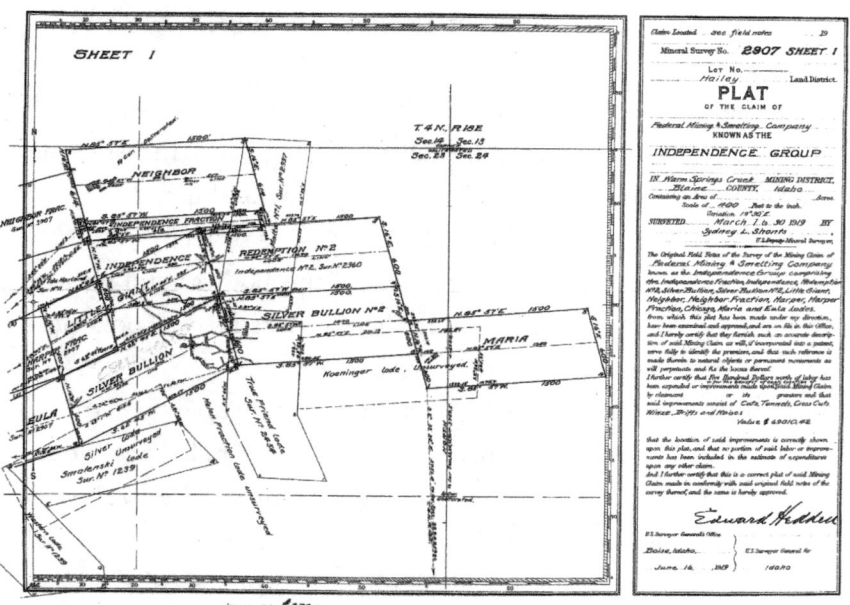

"This is the end of the company's private property. The rest of this land is federal and we lease it," he said.

"You talk like you own the place."

She sure was cute, he thought. "I wish. I love this mountain. It's full of silver and it's a good job. Good jobs are hard to find." He was shifting gears. "Hey, these next claims are all unpatented, that means they belong to the government, but we get to mine them for a fee, based on our production. These days, it all pays the same 'cause the government fixes the price and that's that. These claims are called the Annie Group. There're about fifty claims, almost 1,000 acres with your name on it," he said with a smile.

"I like that. A mountain with my name on it." She pushed off again and he tailed her.

They came down 1,000 feet of cleared, high ground and then passed through a group of Aspen trees. There they picked up a work road, more like a cut, that lead them out of the trees and onto the last, long descent to the creek at the bottom of the valley.

"Watch out for the elk shit, it's everywhere in here."

They could smell the herd just yards away. Over a hundred large animals tend to pack things down some.

The two adventurers trekked the rest of the distance to a little parking area where a '34 Ford sat with several other cars. The keys were left in it, in fact, the keys were in every car.

They unstrapped their skies, climbed in the pickup and headed back the two miles to the rail head.

There, they got in the company truck and he drove her back to the dorms.

When they got there, they sat in the truck for a bit and talked. Then he kissed her. She was a good kisser and they practiced for a while before she put the brakes on and said good night.

"When can we do this again?" ole puppy eyes asked.

"The skiing or the kissing?" She gave him a big smile.

"Both," he said.

"I'm off again next Monday. I might be able to get you a guest pass on Dollar Mountain."

When Rowdey brought the truck back to the fitting shop, Rutter was sitting in his favorite chair, his feet up on the Coke machine.

"Well," Rutter's English accent was still hard for Rowdey to get over, "the prodigal son returns from the rut."

"What rut?" said Rowdey.

Jack pressed on, "I called Donald down at the garage. He told me you picked up the truck almost five hours ago and you were driving around town with the fair lass from Princeton. In over your head, sonny boy, that one's too high up the food chain for you." Jack was enjoying this. "Then I get a call from the mill at the Independence and you're riding the cable with guests, that's stretching things some now, don'tcha think?"

"Aw, c'mon, Jack," the cowboy was on the defensive now. "I was off the clock and she was a good skier. We had no problems jumpin' the tram."

"I bet you didn't," a low, deeper voice was followed by a flush as Rupert came out of the water closet, cinching his belt. "What gives you the right to take a company truck on a lark with a woman? Have you gone mad, do you think we have time to go save your butt up there if she was to fall and get hurt?" Rupe pretended to be angry

"You're just pissed 'cause she gave you a beating in 8 ball. Besides, I think I'm in love." The cowboy was in too deep to quit now.

"Oh, shit," the two guys chimed in surprise.

"What makes you think a Princeton girl who studies -- what was it, Rupe?" Jack turned to Rupe. "Bio mechanics?"

"Biochemical Engineering," Rupe said.

They were having way too much fun now.

"I'm going to my cabin." Rowdey pulled his hat down over his forehead. "I gotta get some sleep."

"You better," said Rupe, "you gotta work tonight."

"Son of a gun, we're having some fun with the BIO." They both heckled him as he walked down the gravel road to his little shack by the river.

Chapter Fourteen

The next morning, Ed Swent had his usual engineering meeting in the main room of the office. The big vault door was swung open and a large roll of fabric-reinforced map paper was brought out. This map was 4 feet by 12 feet long and every day the shift bosses would place it on a long table. They would proceed with progress reports from various levels and pencil draw the tunnel advancement from the previous day. The tunnel map was growing in multiple directions every morning

"Men, I got a letter from the Bureau of Mines in Pennsylvania, the Division of Strategic Metals. We have been asked to increase our production, if possible. They are proposing an expansion program to increase mill efficiency. Jack, have you any suggestions on improvement to your operations?

"Yes I do. We could expand the storage capacity of our ore bins. I could double them and that would help some."

"I need more air," Rupe jumped in. "I always need more air," he chanted.

The men all chuckled. The mine ran on air, Compressors were stationed around that were powered by gasoline engines and then hoses ran down to the worksite. The drills used a lot of cubic feet of air to run all the teams at work within the 90 miles of tunnels.

"We have purchased some used electric compressors from a contractor in Nevada. They were used on the Boulder Dam

Project. They are big, Jack. You're going to have to rebuild the compressor room and will need a cooling tower.

Swent had Rupert's attention now. "How many horsepower?" Jack questioned.

"Over 400. General Electric motors, Worthington Compressors. They're big, Jack, over 30 tons of iron."

The men were actually excited. Air equipment runs poorly when the pressure is insufficient. Crews would struggle with drill bits getting stuck and constant delays. Big air would make life a lot easier down in the hole. Air could run more pumps faster and "the Strike" was getting wider every day.

Now the big boss, Uncle Sam, wanted more, but he was going to pay a little less. The company had no choice in the matter. When they signed on to the Strategic Metals Program, a matter they also had no choice in, they basically agreed that the resources in that mine were the property of the US government.

The government took the silver and gold for the treasury and printed paper money and notes that would be backed by the sovereign or king's metal.

The system was pegged to the British pound, and that was pegged to the LMU or Latin Monetary Union set by Napoleon.

Things jumped around some and considerable blood was shed over changes to the rates, but basically, from the time Maria Theresa's great tits graced the Thaler in Austria, gold was about sixteen times more valuable than silver.

But they wanted the lead. Why, Jack wondered.

Jack was a man of letters and a Freemason. He had studied the life of Newton and was aware of his work stabilizing the coinage of England. England was very concerned about the armies on the move in Europe.

After the morning engineering meeting it was customary for the various bosses to have lunch at the company store. Jack kept his little notebook there and liked to hold court around the coke machine. There was a big electric radiator and good lights. They would often have the *Engineering and Mining Journal* or *Popular Science* open to a story.

"We should've never got off the gold standard," said Swent. "They are just going to print paper and not back it, you watch, you mark my words." He was building up steam for a soap box speech.

Rowdey sashayed in. "I couldn't sleep," he said, expecting the ribbing that was sure to follow. But when the guys didn't mention his escapades, he knew something was up. "What's going on?" he said.

"New equipment coming, big compressors, more production, less money. Government is talking about calling in silver, going to just paper, putting less silver in the coins, same shit as always. They dilute the money supply so we feel like we got more, but we get coins of tin and paper with no backing." Swent was agitated now.

"I hear they need lead more than silver now," said Rowdey. "See, it's here in the *Popular Science*. TEL takes aircraft to new heights. They can't fly without lead, they are running fuels now approaching 90 octane."

"Well, they ain't paying us shit for lead. They don't want us to produce gold, and if it wasn't for our zinc, they would just shut us down. I don't get it," said Rupe.

"I do," said Jack. "About every 100 years or so, the heads of states in Europe kill the Jewish money lenders and erase the debts. They use the Church, or the Devil, or a plague. They always come up with something. Our company controls too

50

much raw material and our government wants it, so it's got off the gold standard to print notes backed by our taxes." Jack was way over everybody's head on this one "They take our silver and print paper, but how do you know how much paper they print for every ounce they hold? You don't, there could be nothing but clay bricks in Fort Knox. We know nothing. But I'll tell ya this, were gonna see a war and things are going to change."

"They will need lead more than silver," said Swent.

"Unless they can make silver bullets," said Rowdey.

"Rupe, can I show Annie "the Strike" sometime? She said she could visit on any Monday." Rowdey expected some flak, but to his surprise, Rupe had no problems with it.

"See that she gets a good lamp and helmet," he said. "And make sure she gets a clean pair of coveralls from the shower room. We are gentlemen here at the Triumph."

Chapter Fifteen

Averell Harriman was contemplating his ski area promotion program, a huge Hollywood production. He had met a young man at a downtown soiree and was expecting him.

His office phone rang, it was Carla. "Mr. Harriman, there's a Mr. Art Arthur here to see you."

"Send him in." Averell was hoping this young writer wrote as good as he talked.

"Mr. Harriman, glad to see you," Art said. "What can I do for you?"

The young writer was a reporter for *The Brooklyn Daily Eagle* and had developed a fair reputation around the Broadway set. Bunny had also heard good things about him.

"Well, Mr. Arthur, how do you feel about winter?"

This was a strange question. "Winters… Mr. Harriman, oh, I guess I like 'em fine: skating in the park, snowmen, fur coats. Sure, I love winter. Why do you ask?" Art was all ears.

Averell stood up and looked out from his office at the New York skyline. "Art, we want to make a movie in our new Shangri-La. We are calling it Sun Valley. It will be a musical. I want all the best people Broadway can send us. I want a big band, like Glenn Miller, some stars and I want it to be the happiest place on earth. Lord knows people can use some happiness these days with all the problems in this world. I've heard good things about you, Art. You've done well here in New

York and we want this to be a big production, nothing but the best. We've talked with Ira Katzenberg and he says you are our man." Averell was on a roll.

Art was glad he had written nothing but glorious reviews on every show Katzenberg was involved in. Today it was all paying off. But he had heard about Claudette Colbert's flop of a comedy *I Met Him in Paris*, filmed in Sun Valley a few years earlier. What a bomb. But, there were rumors about some great parties out there off-set that got pretty wild. Just rumors, he thought. That's how it was on the Great White Way, back-stabbing or back-biting. If Katzenberg recommended him, he had better take it.

"Like an Ice Capade?" Art said. "Like a huge Ice Capade with a story line…"

"Yes," said Averell, "a story of love and song and a hopeful future. I want it to pack our hotel. We have a special train that goes right to Sun Valley. We have the first cable chair that will whisk skiers to a beautiful Lodge atop a fantastic mountain. I want you to go there as soon as you can, what's your schedule?" Averell was a man of action.

"I'm tied up with prior commitments for the next two weeks. I could go there in January." Art said. "Is that soon enough?"

"No, I need you there sooner. I'll pay you well. Try to make some adjustments to your calendar." Averell was pushing. "In the meantime, start working the street. Carla has a contract for you to sign with an advance. Go find Glenn Miller and get him on board and start going to the park and watch the skaters. We are talking with some skaters right now that we know from the Lake Placid Games. You need to make this big. Got it, Art? Could you do this for me?" Averell was piling it on now.

Carla knocked on the door and broke in, "Averell, Baron von Tippelskirch is here for his eleven o'clock." It was only 10:45 a.m. She gave him a look that let him know to wrap this up.

"Call Prescott and get him down here," Averell said. "Arthur, you do your magic. Carla has your contracts. We will talk."

"Okay." Art couldn't be happier. His mind was running at full speed. "Thank you, sir. I will get right on it." And he got up and walked out.

"Carla," Averell picked up his desk phone, "Make sure he signs the contracts and cashes his check at Union Bank this morning, and get Prescott." The urgency on it all was obvious.

"Yes, sir. Mr. Bush is at the Union Board meeting. They said they will be done at eleven-thirty." She was peddling as fast as she could.

"Well, get him out now! This is more important. Tell him I need him up here."

Averell had placed Prescott in a sensitive position of dealing with IG Farben's huge investments in American industry through the Anglo-German Friendship Society.

The baron was the top man for the German armament machine and that machine was running at full throttle. General Motors was producing British aircraft engines in a joint venture with Packard and Pontiac while their Opal division was building heavy trucks for Germany's military.

Brown Brothers Harriman was the banking conduit for the cash, as well as the raw material and chemical production. They sat on the boards of dozens of the biggest players on the world stage. And the world stage was about to draw the curtain on a really big show --a show they would call World War II.

Chapter Sixteen

"Can I get you some coffee, Baron?" Carla was cute enough to stall anybody and she was up to the task.

"I would love some coffee, Madam." The baron stood up and bowed and offered his hand so he could follow with a kiss, like she was a queen or something.

Carla brushed him off with style. "Oh, now, Mr. von Tippelskirch, you don't have to be so formal, this isn't the Champs-Elysees. This is New York."

She was working her room now, she bent over to pour his coffee and he was watching her every move. "Do you take cream?" She gave him a big smile.

"I would like to take you to lunch." The baron was a confident fellow. "I want to see this place they call Sardi's." He couldn't take his eyes off her and would be happy for a delay of his meeting with Averell. He fully understood he had arrived early, unannounced, and there was some scrambling going on.

Carla was doing a little dance, the slow peddle, and he liked it. She did too. It was one of her best routines.

"Oh, Sardi's is too far Uptown, Baron. We would never make it back," she winked.

"That would be wonderful, we would not come back." Now it had just broken into a full-on flirt. "What would you tell your husband?" The baron was throwing a long pass and to his surprise, she caught it.

"Oh, Baron, now you are being fresh," she put out her ring finger and flicked it like the little bird she was. "Nobody has given me a diamond," and she made a little pout.

"You poor child," he said. "We shall have to rectify that."

The hook was set, but by whom?

Just then the elevator doors opened and Prescott came into the outer office. The baron quit his playing and shifted gears.

"Baron von Tippelskirch, I'm Prescott Bush, welcome to Brown Brothers Harriman. Did you have a good trip?" Prescott put his arm across the baron's shoulder and the two men moved toward the polished brass door to Averell's office.

Averell was seated behind his sprawling desk, appointed with a lighter from Tiffany's, a leather pad and a desk lamp, also from Tiffany's, and a gold pen.

The wall behind him had some portraits and railroad paintings by Remington. And in the middle of the room, set upon a specially-built table, was a large model of his Sun Valley resort.

Prescott sat the baron in a leather chair to the right, with a view of the lower Manhattan skyline.

Averell offered the baron a light, "To what do we owe this occasion, Baron?" Averell was not expecting him at all. "I had heard you were in Boston."

"We need a special procurement of a large amount of Tetraethylene, Mr. Harriman. We are making TEL at our plants with the help of our Standard Oil affiliates, but we don't have adequate supply of the raw materials required to produce enough for our expanding demands."

Averell and Prescott were both well aware of what the expanding demands meant. Charles Lindbergh had just returned from a world-wind tour of the aircraft plants in both England

and Germany and had written a letter to the War Department that Averell chaired, explaining the levels of German aircraft production as compared to the British. It was pitiful, even with the Packard-Pontiac agreement on Rolls- Royce engines, the German production output was thirty times that of the British, much of it owed to IG Farben's friends at the Anglo-German Friendship Society.

The baron puffed the cigar, took a look at the Cuban label and flicked his ashes in the tray on the table. "I need to secure a large amount of the highest quality aviation fuel and a large quantity of Tetraethylene lead," the baron was a very confident man who got what he wanted.

"How much are we talking about?" said Prescott.

"Five hundred thousand barrels of aviation gasoline with an octane rating of 90. And 500 tons of Tetraethylene lead. I trust you can deliver those quantities to your friends in Germany. I have heard rumors of an embargo from your president."

"I have heard those rumors too, Baron," said Averell. "Rest assured, we will have your orders filled."

"Thank you." The baron stood up and looked at the model of Sun Valley. "What is this here?" He asked, having a love for the mountains.

"This is our new ski area out west, Baron. Are you a skier?" Averell loved talking about his development. It was far away, like an escape of sorts. He knew what was coming.

"Of course. I love to ski," said the baron. "I grew up not far from Garmisch. I have run the Kandahar downhill many times as a boy. We have very good snow in Garmisch."

The two men broke from the business at hand, to a better topic that they both would rather deal with.

"You must come to Idaho, Baron." Averell was seeing a good opportunity for a much needed break. In fact, your order for TEL begins there in one of our mines." Averell was suddenly on the pitch. "You could wire your office and tell them you need to make an inspection of the raw material supply." Averell smiled half-jokingly.

"I don't need to receive permission to ski," the baron seemed affronted some.

"No, no, of course not," Averell steered clear of any friction. So you'll come. We can fly out next week."

"Of course," said the German. "I'm staying at the Pennsylvania."

"I know," said Averell. It was his hotel. "My secretary will send you the details. Tuesday, weather-permitting, we will fly out. We can be back in a week, get you home by Christmas. Is that good?" Averell was looking forward to some skiing.

The meeting ended and the baron left the office, tipping his hat to Carla, and taking the elevator down.

As he exited the building, he walked right next across the street to 38 Wall Street and entered Tiffany's.

Within an hour, a courier was at Carla's desk with a little, sky blue box and a card that read: *Sardi's 7:00 p.m.* The box had a Victory brilliant-cut tennis bracelet, over six carats.

Carla was invited to dinner. Her mind began to race. She couldn't accept a gift like this from a man she met one time for a few minutes, could she? This was a big ticket item with strings, heavy strings, attached. She was looking down at the sparkling gift that was still in its box on her desk, when her phone rang.

"Mr. Harriman's office," she answered.

"Carla Green?" A voice on the other end asked.

"Yes, this is she. Who is this?" She rarely received personal calls on this line and wondered how this call got past the switchboard.

"My name is Shoup. I understand that you have a large bracelet that was just delivered."

Carla was suddenly both surprised and alarmed with this call.

"Who are you and what do you want? How do you know what is on my desk?"

"Miss Green, there is not much about a large diamond purchase in New York that I don't know about." Shoup was careful not to scare her. "The man that was in your office is of great concern to me and my people, your people, Miss Grunspan."

"Who the hell is this?" She was angry now. "How do you know my father's name?"

"My father knew your father in the old country," he said calmly. "They worked together. They did business together. They sat together in Temple." Mr. Shoup seemed very sincere. "That bracelet was bought with blood money and that man is a dangerous man," Shoup continued. "We want your help."

What had begun as a normal day was turning into a runaway train. Carla's mother never spoke of her father much. They came to New York in 1921. Carla was a baby and her mother a widow with some money. She made sure her daughter was Americanized. She took an English name and put her in a private school. She was brought up with a business education and her mother seldom spoke of the old country. Carla knew that her father ran a Yiddish newspaper in Russia and was killed by a group called the Cheka, that's all. Her mother escaped Russia and made it to New York. Carla Grunspan became Carla

Green and tonight she was going to dinner. She pulled the bracelet out of the box and clipped it on her wrist.

"What do you want me to do?" She said.

Chapter Seventeen

The next day, Federal Mining and Smelting in Salt Lake City received an extra order from DuPont for 500 tons of lead. Within a few days, it was on flat car with a much bigger order, making its way to Penns Grove, New Jersey. Some of it had been blasted from "the Strike" at the Triumph, just a few weeks earlier.

Chapter Eighteen

Posey and her husband, Ted, built a fine cabin way up Baker Creek, north of Ketchum, that they called Chalet Vengreen. It was used in the set of a B movie called *I Met Him In Paris* with Claudette Colbert in 1937.

The film company built a mock-up Swiss village and there was a rope tow up on Vengreen Mountain.

Not far from there, a hot springs bubbled up from deep in the earth and a small pool about 10 feet across and 3 feet deep sent a cloud of steam into the cold winter night.

The Boulder Mountains rose up like a giant wall of shimmering rock 10,000 feet high.

It was this pool that first drew Ted and Posey to this place as lovers, in 1935. Few places on earth could compare to a bath at Baker Creek. Couples could sit and look up at an enormous sky. The high altitude provided crystal clear viewing of the stars. Lovers could sit for hours in the 115 degree water. There were no signs, no markers, just a plume of steam.

Parties at the cabin would often include several like-minded couples, who were not inhibited, always ending up in the pool after a dinner and some drinks. Occasionally, someone might bring some opium or marijuana.

After an hour or two of liberal activity and conversation, the group would trek back the mile or so to the big fire in the cabin.

These parties soon became the talk of a very exclusive set of Hollywood stars and starlets and some very powerful politicos from New York. Several of the Austrian ski instructors would often show up and act as guides, for those luminaries that couldn't ski well.

As the word traveled through the grapevine, people like Papa Hemingway and Lucille Ball might show up. The private ski experience on a full-moon night became legendary.

These parties were usually a weekend affair. During the week, nobody was ever out there.

It was a Monday night, just a three-quarter moon and Rowdey convinced Annie to go on a night ski. "Bring a rucksack and a cotton towel," he said.

"Towel? What for?" Her antennae were up.

"In case we go swimming," he joked.

"It's 10 degrees," she said. "Just in case, maybe a small Lodge blanket."

The Lodge had short, blue blankets made by the Pendleton Woolen Mills of Oregon. Annie put one in her pack, with a towel, some cheese, an apple, and a small flask of peach port.

Rowdey picked her up at five in the company truck. He told Jack what he was up too and the boss told him to be careful and have a good time. He promised he would be. And the two motored up Route 94 on a brisk, clear December evening.

The sun was still shining on the very peaks of the Boulders as the one ton, with two pairs of skies and two small packs on the bed, carried the two young lovers to a mountain paradise.

The truck pulled into the Baker Creek turnoff. Rowdey hung the keys under the hood on the throttle cable. This was no place to lose your keys on a winter night. There would be nobody

64

coming out this road. The two strapped on the bear traps, ski bindings and began trekking on out toward Mount Vengreen.

They would climb for about a half hour, and then ski down a mile to the hot pool. Of course, Annie had no idea there was a bath waiting for her out here. Rowdey had made this risky decision based on the heavy petting and good kissing that had occurred previously. It was an acceptable risk and he took it.

As the two skied down the hill, a small plume of the pool steam rose up in front of them.

"Wow," said Annie. "You weren't kidding about a swim." She had spent many weekends in Vermont and was familiar with the whole sauna, hot pool thing.

To Rowdey's surprise, she was quickly getting her gear off and pulling out the blanket. They packed down an area with their skies alongside the pool. The snow was deep and damp, because of the steam, and it quickly made a stable, icy platform.

The young couple set their gear down and disrobed with the winter chill at their back and the steaming pool calling them in. They were young, strong, and beautiful. All the night sky played for them and them alone as they embraced life and each other.

Chapter Nineteen

Teterboro Airport, December 15[th,] 1938, the DC-2 was outfitted with the latest comforts and equipment. Averell made sure everything was good to go and had an entourage of twelve people headed out for a ski vacation to remember.

Most were accomplished skiers with lots of experience in New York and Vermont. His second wife, Marie Norton Whitney, Anaconda Copper president, Cornelius Kelley, along with the Baron von Tippelskirch, Carla, Joe Widener from the Belmont Track, and Bunny and Margie.

It was a mixed bag of folks and potential investors in The Sun Valley Company, as well as the writers for what would become the movie *Sun Valley Serenade,* Mack Gordon and his actress friend, Ann Doran, composer Harry Warren, his friends pianist Eddy Duchin, and Duri Alexander.

The plane made its way across the country, stopping in St. Louis and Denver for fuel.

The trip took fourteen hours, and luckily the weather was very good, and the sky was clear when the plane touched down on the runway, south of Ketchum at Gimlet.

The Sun Valley Stage Bus was waiting for the group at the hanger and they were quickly on the way to the big fireplace in the grand lobby of the Lodge.

The place was abuzz with activity. The bar was packed, a five-piece house band was working and the dance floor was full.

The staff swarmed over Averell's party and took their bags to rooms scattered around the four wings of the upper floors.

Carla knew her way around and led the baron to his room. Much to his disappointment, she had her own room up the hall.

"I'll freshen up, darling, and see you down in the lounge in a hour," she gave him a little peck. Carla was always working and the baron knew it. She was wearing the diamonds he bought her.

He retired. It had been a long flight. The room was very comfortable, though smaller than the rooms in the hotels of the Alps that he was used to.

As he looked out the window from the third floor of the west wing, he could see the magnificent hot pool with the steam billowing up in the cold, night air.

He got out of his travel clothes, grabbed the terry cloth robe that was hanging in the bath and made his way down the stairwell, following the signs that pointed to the pool.

When he arrived at the pool's guest counter, he was greeted by an attractive young woman who gave him a locker room key and a house bathing suit with the Sun Valley logo embossed on the band.

"Enjoy your evening," said Annie, as she gave the baron a big smile.

Annie had begun working an evening shift at the pool two days a week. It was better than housekeeping, and there were tips.

The baron went into the locker room and put on the trunks, then he locked his money clip and his waterproof Rolex watch in his locker and walked out to the pool. The evening temperature was now below zero and the hot pool's fog was so thick he could hardly see the water.

There were lights under the surface that lit up the stairs into the large pool. The pool was over 50 feet around with a brown concrete wall and big glass panels enclosing the whole complex, but open to the stars.

It was magnificent. The baron had never seen anything like it. He got into the pool and made his way towards the center. The water felt great. The steam rose up all around him. At the far side of the pool, he could just make out the face of a woman, as he moved closer, he saw it was Carla.

"Hello, stranger," she said, summoning him towards her.

She was beautiful and she had a power over him he couldn't control. She put her hands on his shoulders and began to give him a massage.

"You must be tense from all this big business you have going on," she said as she pressed herself against his body. She backed away some when he tried to kiss her. She wasn't ready for that— yet. But after working his shoulders, she slid her manicured hand over his trunks, lightly, just enough to give him an idea of more, but just that: an idea.

She held him from behind and the two were still in the hot water for about five minutes, then Carla gently pushed off and swam to the stairs. She climbed out of the pool, wrapping a robe around her shapely figure.

"I'll meet you in the lounge in an hour, Baron," she said, as she went back into the hotel.

He didn't respond. He was thinking about his home of Garmisch. There was nothing like this there. He was beginning to like this place. Who wouldn't with a gal like Carla around. But, Kurt von Tippleskirsch was a 41-year-old man with a wife and family back in Germany. He was here in America procuring fuel supplies for what would be the largest, single land war with the heaviest losses and the most horrible atrocities ever inflicted by man against his fellow man.

Right now, in this place, a beautiful woman was toying with him, the water was hot, the air was clean, and the battle field was 8,000 miles round the globe. Plus, tomorrow, he would be skiing. He knew very well that it might be his last time and he was going to make the best of it.

He stayed in the hot pool for another twenty minutes. It was empty. The sound from the dance band in the bar echoed around the huge building. People were dancing and laughing. He heard all this from the stillness of the pool.

The pool attendant sat at her desk in the hallway reading a magazine. This place was a big land with a big sky, the kind of land that his Fuhrer spoke of in his speeches about German re-colonization.

After Germany wins the war in Europe, they will take over this land too, he thought. Perhaps his Fuhrer would allow him to run this place. He would like that. But he knew better than anyone else, without lead, Germany's rolling and flying stock would be worthless.

At about 11:30 p.m., the baron pulled himself up the stairs and out of the pool. He wrapped himself in the terry cloth robe, said good night to Annie, still at the counter, and made his way up the stairs to his room. Within a minute of hitting the sheets, he was out like a light.

Carla put on a pair of jeans and a red ski sweater that she had just bought at Macy's before she left New York. She retrieved a packet of matches she was given by a waiter at Sardi's the night she was there with the baron for dinner.

Inside was written the words: *Mr. Shoup, The Jewish Daily Record,* and a phone number, *Murray Hill 7-2559.*

Carla went down to the phone booths in the Lodge lobby and dialed. It was two in the morning in New York and the press room would be abuzz with the printing of *The Daily*.

"Press Room," a voice on the other end of the line with a thick, Yiddish accent said.

"Mr. Shoup?" Carla asked.

"Speaking." Shoup said.

"The baron is in Sun Valley. The lead sale is approved. I have his confidence. What do you want me to do?"

"Kill the son of a bitch." Shoup didn't hesitate.

"I'm not trained for that. I can collect information. You'll need to get someone else here to do that." She said.

"We have someone there already." Shoup said. "He is an Austrian exile and he will contact you. Stay with the baron, earn his trust. And Miss Grunspan, we thank you. Be careful." He hung up the phone.

As Carla moved down the Lodge hallway to the bar, she could hear Harry Warren and Eddy Duchin at the piano playing the popular Gershwin melody, *Rhapsody in Blue*.

Harry's real name was Salvatore Antonio Guaragna, a wop. His buddy, Eddy Duchin, was a Jew. Eddy's parents had fled Bessarabia, a special area set up by Tzar Nicholas for Jewish merchants who were given tax breaks and were so successful, that by 1900, the Christian population was envious of their wealth.

In 1903, a young Christian boy was murdered and the local Jews were falsely accused. A bloodbath followed and Eddy's parents had to flee. They arrived in New York in the spring of 1906 and Eddy was born soon after.

The two, young men, four magic hands, danced on the big Baldwin Grand, ringing out the quintessential American tune.

While just a few miles away, 800 feet into an Idaho mountain, a quantity of lead ore was being extracted that would fuel a mad man's army and would change the face of the land their parents left forever.

Annie finished her night shift at the Lodge pool and went back to her room above the Inn. There she got out of her company uniform --that looked like something out of Mother Hubbard's nursery rhymes-- and put on her lined, blue jeans and a heavy sweatshirt with a turtle neck. Tonight she was getting a tour of the Triumph Mine workings.

This was her third date. She and Rowdey were in over their heads. She hadn't slept with him. But she took a bath with him. She liked him a lot, but she knew she would be going back east to take a research job next fall with Alice Hamilton at Harvard, in the field of Industrial Workplace Exposure. Workplace toxicology was Doc Hamilton's forte. Little did Rowdey know how much Annie was looking forward to this mine tour.

She waited for her date in front of the Lodge as the guests came and went. A long, black Cadillac limousine purred up to the big portico and the doormen swept over it, helping out Posey, her husband, Ted, and Simone, the manager of The Alpine Bar, and a young reporter named Ernest, from New York.

Simone and Ernest had already consumed a fair amount of scotch and needed to prop each other up to make it in the door. It was a big night at the Lodge and Averell made sure everyone who was anyone knew that some fine piano players from the Great White Way were in town. His publicity machine had taken care of it all. The hotel staff was on notice, it was to be a special event.

71

As Posey's driver, George, pulled the big, twelve-cylinder Caddy out, a black and white Chevy truck with the words *Triumph Mining Co.--not for hire* written in simple, small stenciled letters, pulled in.

Annie jumped in with a smile. She was punching out. "Let's get out of here." She said. "This place is a mad house tonight."

The two rolled out down Sun Valley Road and then up the East Fork of the Big Wood River. The half moon was enough to light up the Pioneers and reflected on their snow-covered peaks. They were magnificent. Annie couldn't see them from Sun Valley and she had no idea that such a beautiful mountain range was so close.

They pulled into the town of Triumph and Rowdey showed her into the mining company office. The noon shift would be punching out soon. Rowdey gave Annie a clean pair of gray striped coverall. He then strapped a thick, leather belt around her waist that carried a battery pack and had a thin wire that ran to the headlamp on a brown helmet. Then he handed her a pair of cloth work gloves.

"Put these on and follow me. Here, put these cotton balls in your ears. It gets a little noisy through these doors."

She followed him through a series of small rooms filled with supplies and when he opened the last door into the mill, the noise was deafening.

Large wheels with leather belts ran the length of the long work room. They climbed the stairs past the shaker tables and up towards the stamp machines. Annie put her hand over her ears, *it was loud!*

They exited on top of the building, up one more set of stairs, past a large, wooden water tank, to the tram room.

Here, the tram cars dumped their load into hoppers that fed the stamp crushers.

It was so loud here, as well, that Rowdey didn't try to explain what was going on, but it was pretty easy to see what was happening.

"At the top of the mill here..." Rowdey tried, it was still loud, but not as bad. "The high-grade ore is broken into dust. Then it moves by gravity and water to the shaker tables that separate the heavier materials. The heavy material is called the concentrate and we send that to the smelter."

He took her by the arm and they headed toward the bucket cars. "Now these are a little bigger than the others, but they move along, so be ready to hop in, okay?"

Annie shook her head in acknowledgment and the two hopped in a car headed up to the North Star Mine.

At the top of the tram was another large, barn-looking building. Here, they off-loaded and walked through a cook house that could seat and feed fifty men, past a change room with more lockers, and then into the Plummer tunnel.

"This is our main tunnel," said Rowdey. It was very quiet and still in this mountain. "This tunnel is 4,500 feet long and it comes out on the other side of the mountain. It's a pretty good walk. Can you see okay?"

He checked her light and her belt and gave her a little squeeze.

"Ever make out in a tunnel?" He held her close.

"Save it." She said. "Nothing turns a girl off more than striped coveralls."

"What, these things are great, they have long zippers." He eyed her up and down.

"Get real, keep walking. I can see fine. I'm right behind you and I'm watching your every move."

The two proceeded into the Plummer tunnel. It was large enough for a small car to drive through. There were two-inch iron pipes on the right side of the path and a set of steel tracks, like a little train would use, up the center. Everything was very neat and solid.

Up ahead, she could see lights and hear some workmen talking. They had walked about a half mile when they came to an intersection.

"This is a raise," Rowdey pointed up a long sloping passage. "This connects with a higher-level tunnel that goes all the way back to the Independence, where we skied last week. It's over a mile. The air is very good in this mine because it rises through the mountain like hot air in a chimney. Some mines have rotten air, but we are lucky." Rowdey took her hand and led her on towards the workmen.

As they got closer to the lights of the crew ahead, Annie could hear rocks and shovels and the sound of an air-powered mucker. They came into a big, shiny cavern. It was huge.

"This is 'the Strike'," said Rowdey. He was puffed up some, as he should be. "This is one of the largest silver strikes ever found, anywhere." Rowdey had his arms up like a conductor in a symphony. "It's over 700 feet long and 50 feet tall. This month we will be the largest producer of zinc in America and the number two producer of silver. The silver in this ore runs about 20 ounces per ton. It's mixed with the lead. The lead pays the rent, but the silver buys the groceries..."

He pulled a piece of high-grade ore from the ore cart the men had loaded. It was about the size of a baseball. It was so heavy Annie had to strain to hold it up.

"Wow." She was surprised at its weight. "It wouldn't take much of this to make a ton."

"Yea, I know." Rowdey chuckled. "That big, ole dump truck they use to haul it to the rail head can only put about a foot of the concentrate in its bed and the tires start to go flat."

"Are you at all worried about handling lead? You know it's somewhat dangerous." She thought she was giving him information he would not be aware of.

"Not at all." He was glad she gave him a stumper. "This is galena. It's not water-soluble, it's very safe, but if it mixes with acid, like some of the sulfides that form when some of these rocks rust, then you could get a visit from the Tommy Knockers." He smiled at her. He was in his element here.

"Tommy Knockers?" She thought he was pulling her leg. "What are Tommy Knockers?"

"They are little ghosts in the mountain that talk to ya. If you don't wash the red oxide off ya or get some in your lunch pail, you might get a visit from the Tommy Knockers."

"I think you've been hit in the head by a Tommy Knocker." She was sure he was kidding her now.

"Well, okay, go on, make fun of me, but you see that foam looking stuff growing on that rusty rock up there?" He pointed his headlamp up to a rock face across from "the Strike". The rocks were wet and dripping with this cream-colored, fungus, mushroom-like stuff. "Go grab some of that stuff and put it on your crackers," he sounded serious. "You get a visit from the Tommy Knockers."

Like the Mad Hatter in *Alice In Wonderland*." She said. "We studied the effects on the human brain in chemistry, that's my field of study -- Industrial Hazards in the Workplace."

"Are you telling me you've been using me to gain access to my workplace? I feel used, like a lab rat." Rowdey pretended to pout.

"You're a little cuter than a lab rat." She said. "It's been shown that exposure to certain chemicals can have strange effects on the human body. I'll tell you about it later." She took a long look around at the huge cavern and began to climb up the ladder towards the face.

"Whoa," said Rowdey. "Where do you think you're going? We just don't climb wherever we want to down in here. We have procedures."

"I want a sample of that foamy stuff," she pointed her finger in the direction of a fungus that looked like tan shaving cream hanging down about two inches from a particularly rusty looking vein of rock with yellow and black streaks.

"Just hold on." He put his hand on her arm. "I'll get you some of that stuff, it's everywhere. You don't need to be climbing up those timber sets."

The timber sets were almost 50 feet tall, built like a post and beam barn, except they were wedged-in in many places and as the mountain would move ever so slowly, the miners would hammer the wedges tighter, when needed, to keep everything in tension.

"Where do you get all this wood?" She looked down from the first platform she had scampered up on. "It looks like you cut down a whole forest."

"Actually, most of this wood came off your ski mountain when they cleared the trails this summer, but we get it from all over, north of here, where we were last week in the pool." He gave her a little wink. "Come on down," he motioned.

"Better get your lady friend down from the sets," the deep voice of the big boss man bellowed from a tunnel behind them as Rupert made himself known to the guest.

Annie came down off the first of five levels of timbered sets that filled in all the voids in the cavernous workings.

"We like having visitors down in here, but they need to stay with the guide and it's up to the guide to keep it that way." He raised his eyebrow at Rowdey.

"Okay, boss, I'll keep her on a tighter leash." He smiled back and waved Annie down.

"We have two sawmills on the mountain and they never stop," said Rupert. "Everything needs to be timbered. We have strict safety procedures that we follow."

The two realized that their conversation had been overheard by the boss.

Down in the mountain, Rupe was boss, and he had a matter of fact confidence that let you know it. But he loved to flirt with the ladies and seldom was a pretty lady present in his mountain, so like it or not, the tour just got bigger.

"Rule number one I try to follow is, we don't eat nothing down here unless it's wrapped in tin foil and comes out of our lunch pail," he smiled at Annie as he looked up at the red, iron veins.

"Anybody want some cake? Bonnie packed me enough for a small army," he motioned to an iron, tool box and a board set on two timber blocks that made a little resting area.

"Step into my office," he said, as Annie brushed off her coveralls that had gotten covered with a reddish brown slime when she crawled up the timber sets.

"Now you see why we don't just crawl anywhere, that red oxide is messy and there's no need to drag it back to the wash tub."

He opened the iron tool box and pulled out a black lunch box with a half-round lid that flipped up. In the lid was a thermos of coffee, and in the box, there was a couple of sandwiches and two big pieces of chocolate cake--each wrapped in shiny tin foil that flickered in the light of the miners lamps on their brown helmets.

"I always heard the best way to a girl's heart is through her stomach." He smiled as his booming voice could be heard down the tunnel.

Rup was losing his hearing from years around the air drills, but he refused to admit it. He had also had his ears boxed a few too many times as a young-buck, Golden Gloves champ.

He handed Annie a piece of chocolate cake, "Coffee?" he passed the cup from the top of the thermos, and pulled a small white towel out of the tool box.

"Here." He passed it to Annie. "Wipe your hands. We don't want that red junk ruining a good cup of coffee."

"Rule number one," said Annie.

"She's a fast learner," said Rupe, looking at Rowdey. "Maybe we should give her a job."

"No thanks," said Annie. "I think I'll keep my job in that nice, warm, carpeted hotel. She motioned a "thank you" with the coffee cup.

"The iron sulphate mixes with the fresh air from the outside…" Picking up the conversation that the two were into when he interrupted them. "There are some funguses that will grow without light and they need iron to do it."

"They need oxygen," said Annie. "They get it from the iron mixing with the water and air, oxidation. I studied chemistry at Princeton. That stuff is probably producing a mild acid as a by-product and when certain acids get in the body, people can go a little crazy until they work them out, like bread molds and poison mushrooms. Some primitive Indian tribes eat molds to make them have religious hallucinations. This is my field of study. I wrote my paper on the health effects of Tetraethylene lead on the workers at the Standard Oil Company plant in Port Elizabeth, New Jersey."

Annie was on a roll and Rupert put on the brakes.

"How's the cake?" to stop her abruptly. "My wife made it for my son's birthday. I have three kids." Rupe changed the subject. "We have a nice, little house with a pitcher pump right in the kitchen. I drove it down myself into the ground with a sledge."

Annie was getting the message.

"This is a good job here at the Triumph, pays good, it's warm in here," he looked at Annie in a matter of fact kind of way. "We know our minerals. That red iron sulfide will kill a horse in a few years if he drinks the mine water from the flume. We just stay clear of it and keep our dirty hands out of our mouths." He smiled at Annie.

"Good cake," she said. The meeting was over.

"Well," said Rupe, as he shut up the lunch box and placed it back in his tool locker. "Some of us have work to do."

He stood up and stretched. "Enjoy the rest of your tour and don't wander off into a blind tunnel, the Tommy Knockers might get cha'."

He looked her straight in her pretty green eyes. They understood each other. He walked off down the Plummer tunnel.

"What a character," said Annie.

"Yea, he's the real deal. I'm lucky to be working with him." Rowdey crumpled up the tin foil and tossed it in an ore cart filled with shiny silver ore. "Well. Want to see my place? I got a good wood stove and a comfortable chair." He looked at his date with renewed interest.

"I guess I better," she said.

The two started to walk the half mile back to the North Star tram and Rowdey said: "Tell me about this paper you wrote. What's that about?"

"Well, most of this lead here probably ends up in New Jersey. They grind it into dust and cook it in a great big, double kettle with this chemical called ethyl. It's like gin or vodka, they mix the mash in this kettle and bring it to a boil, like beer or whisky, more like whisky, and the steam that condenses from that cooking is called TEL…"

The two walked down between the little rails in the tunnel like a couple of kids walking down a railroad track talking about the World Series or why the sky was blue, just moseying along, in a mountain, enjoying each other's company.

"I know that stuff," he said. "It's octane booster. They need it for aircraft fuel."

"Yep, that's it. Tetraethylene lead, very nasty, killed a lot of men in a factory explosion and they went mad before they died. It was horrible, the worst factory accident in history." She was again in her element. "When they are done cooking this mash, they mix the TEL with gasoline and send the paste to paint manufactures in Newark. We are studying the long-term effects on the human body of these chemicals and researching safer ways of handling them: masks, ventilation, fire prevention, that sort of thing. The airplanes need this stuff to fly, so it's going to be around a while."

When they reached the outside it was cold and clear. They walked down a snowplowed road across the North Star claim to a large, wooden shed that once housed the donkeys in the old days, before air power.

Rowdey rolled back a garage door and there sat a Bantam pickup, dented and battered.

"Jump in," he said and Annie climbed aboard.

The truck fired up. Rowdey checked to make sure the brakes were pumped up and they slowly rolled down the North Star Road that led to the little town of Triumph.

They could see the lights of the village and the wood smoke rising from chimneys that formed a little cloud that hovered in the valley.

"I thought you weren't supposed to use the company truck." She gave him one of those great, questioning smiles.

"This beauty…" He tapped on the dashboard. "This is all mine. Runs good. Doesn't look that good, but it will gets us were we need to go. Want to go to California?"

"Not right now, thank you. I like it right here in Idaho." She patted him on his lap.

The Bantam rolled into town, past the mill and welding shop, and down to a little cabin down by the river: One room, with a bunk, a couple of chairs, and an iron stove. A tail of smoke was just barely making it out of a little, rusty metal pipe sticking out of the roof.

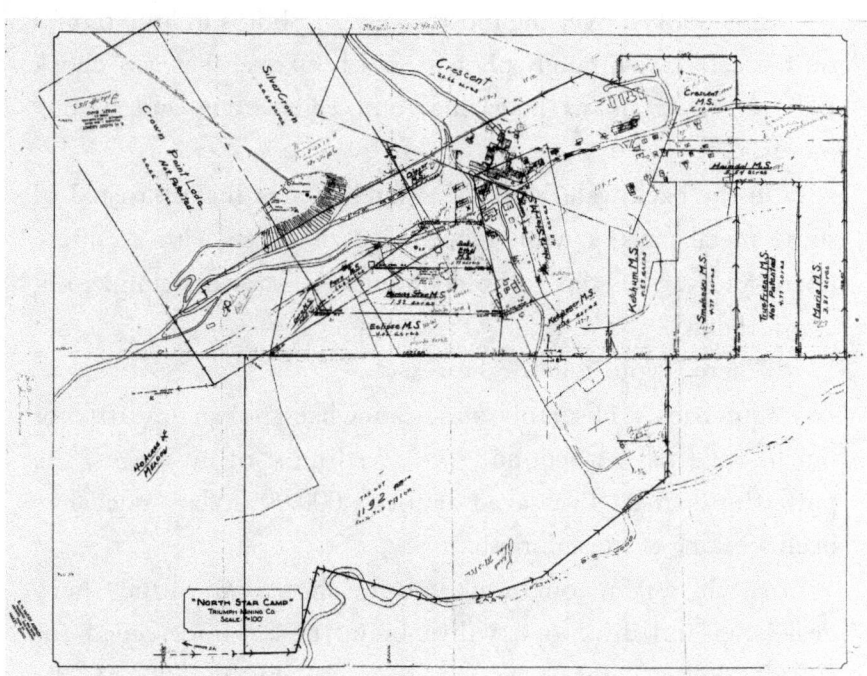

Rowdey swung open the heavy wooden door, struck a stick match, from a holder on the wall, and lit a kerosene lamp. As the glass came down around the little flame, the place lit up with a homey glow. It was clearly a man's place, but it was neat and orderly.

As Annie walked around the little room of this man she was about to spend the night with, he was at the wood stove, stoking the black potbelly until it had a good fire.

He left the air adjuster on the stove open full so the piglet began to chug like a locomotive until the room was warm and comfortable.

He lit two more lamps, on the table and on a nightstand near his bunk.

Annie looked over the mostly western photos in little frames on the cabin wall, family photos on a bookcase that was chock full of *Popular Science* magazines and engineering and mining journals.

On the back wall there was a kitchen area that consisted of some metal pails, a wash tub, a kind of hutch with a cutting board and various tins to hold supplies. It was very simple, but comfortable.

"Where is your toilet?" she asked.

"Out back." His reply was somewhat apologetic "It's not much, but I pay no rent and I've saved most of my wages," he puffed up some. "I've saved almost 1,000.00 dollars since I've been working at the Triumph."

In 1938, a man could walk into the showroom of the Chevy dealership and drive out with a brand new 4-door sedan for 700.00 dollars. For a young man in the middle of the Depression, this was a very respectable sum and Annie couldn't help being a little impressed.

The two lovers had spent a night together at the hot springs, but this was their first night in a real bed, their first of what might be many nights. They both knew it.

They were falling for each other. They began to kiss in front of the wood stove, standing, then they began to unbutton layers of clothing. Soon they both were naked, clutching, and kissing.

They rolled into the bed under a pile of blankets. They made love like they meant it this time.

"It's okay," said Annie. "I'm safe now." And he found himself in her and they both felt like one.

About an hour later, the two were spent and lay side by side in the warm bed. The lights of the lamps flickered, the wood stove had calmed down to a soft ember, it was like the whole room was alive and in unison with them.

The world was perfect until Annie asked the all important question, "So tell me about this toilet out back."

Rowdey knew this was the weak link in his almost perfect lifestyle. He showered and used the flush toilet at the bunk house and seldom had to use the privy, but nature calls.

He jumped out of the bunk and stocked the stove some, then he pulled a long heavy cotton robe off a hook behind the door and motioned to Annie.

"Here, put this on, and take this lamp. It's out the door and to the right, follow the path, you can't miss it."

"I'm sure I won't." She said as she put the robe on.

Living in the most luxurious hotel in the west could certainly spoil a girl. The Lodge was all marble and polished brass. This was rough-sawn lumber and frozen ground, but she was a trooper and it wasn't that bad. She made her first trip to the little shed and came back to the bunk, crawled in beside this man she had known for a month now. There was nobody to judge them.

They were accountable for their own actions and couldn't be more alive.

"What do you want out of life?" She started off the pillow talk easy.

"Oh, I don't know. I like mining. I'd like to run a mill, maybe have my own mill someday. I'd like to see Australia. They say there's fresh mining opportunities there. If we live that long. We're headed right into a war, so who knows." He was fingering her belly button.

"Stop that. It tickles." She pushed his hand away. "I'd like to have a horse and a little farm back in New Jersey," she said. "I can teach at Princeton after I get a Master's and I'll get one after this next job that I start in the spring, up in Boston."

That was a bold statement for a woman to make. Very few women were able to get into the circles of college professorships. But the woman she was studying with was Alice Hamilton, and Alice had hit the glass ceiling with a sledge hammer. After the Bayway disasters at the Standard Oil TEL plant, so many workers went mad that the state shut them down. Miss Hamilton found herself at the forefront of a national industrial disaster.

The pillow talk made it very clear to the two of them, that they were on different paths, but right now, right here, it seemed perfect, almost.

Chapter Twenty

In the morning, Rowdey fired up his truck and ran Annie back to her room. She kissed him goodbye and ran up the back stairs of the Inn, past the steaming cooking pots in the kitchen. The hotel was already up and running full speed. She was assigned to the second floor today in the Sun Valley Lodge.

Being a maid was easy work for a young girl her age, hardly worthy of a master's degree in science, but a welcome break from the East Coast. The Depression was hard on folks, but here, all that seemed so far away, here, everyone was in the mood for a party.

Annie pushed her cart down the hall, from room to room, and could hear someone on the piano in the ballroom.

At 10:30 a.m., the girls took a 15 minute break and Annie nosed her head into the ballroom to see two men with a notebook, a yellow pencil and cups of coffee.

"How 'bout this…" the man on the piano played some chords and then the other man jotted some notes on the pad.

"I think we need a walking intro to set this up," he said. "Do you need to get in here?" He looked at Annie.

"No, sir. I'm sorry. I was just enjoying the piano."

"Do you play?" He said. "Come on in and play us a song." He motioned her in.

"Oh no, sir, I couldn't fraternize with the guests."

"We're not guests. I'm Mack. This is Harry. How do you do?"

"My name is Annie Thatcher." Annie offered her hand to the man at the piano. He shook it.

"Hello, Annie, I'm Harry. Harry Warren. We have been hired to write a song about this place and this morning we are drawing a blank. Play us a song, we could use a break."

Annie was well-equipped for a moment like this. She grew up attending a formal, private girls school in Demarest, New Jersey. The Academy of the Holy Angels was a strict Catholic ladies school that trained women for a proper life and made them ready for marriage, family, and in rare circumstances, college. It was right across the Hudson from the Great White Way and Annie was well-versed in music. She had eight years of classical piano and attended many shows with her classmates. The most controversial of its day was a play about a white man and a woman who was half-black, unheard of in 1935.

Annie had just spent the night with a man in a shack, she had made love to him several times and now she was emptying trash pails and cleaning toilets.

Something snapped in the mind of this young woman who was dressed in a maid's uniform, 3,000 miles from the ropes of a collapsing society that she was tethered to.

"Okay," she said. "I'll play you a song."

She sat down on the polished piano bench that was probably cleaned that very morning by one of her workmates, bumping her butt right up to Harry, who was just a little surprised that his morning's work session was being broken by a hotel maid. Then she cracked her fingers--they had been cleaning toilet seats a moment earlier. Harry gave Mack a look like, "Where did this come from?"

Annie played one of her favorite tunes that pretty much summed up how she was feeling: Gershwin's *I Got Plenty o' Nuttin* from *Porgy and Bess*. And she nailed it.

The big, grand piano boomed in the large sun lit room. Annie's fingers danced on the keys and poured all the emotion her heart was feeling from the past two weeks, this place, her new love, the snow. It was like she was in a whole new world. She had a lousy job, but it was a job. She poured it all into three minutes of music.

"I got plenty of nothing, and nothin's plenty for me…" Said Harry. "Very nice, very nice. Very well done. Georgie couldn't play it better himself." Harry said.

"What are you doing in a place like this?" Mack said. "You're pretty good on the ivories, kiddo."

"Thanks. I came here to ski. Have you tried it?" She was looking at Harry.

"Are you joking? He's from Hoboken. He's lucky if he could ride a sled without busting himself up," Mack jumped in.

"Hey, you're the klutz in this outfit. He can't even tie his shoes without his mother helping him." Harry said.

"You keep my mother out of this."

The clowning continued in an obvious slapstick manner as Annie began to rise. She had to get back to her job.

"Play us another," said Harry.

"No thank you. You should try skiing while you're here though, it will give you a thrill." As she got up she could see Mack scribble *a thrill* on his notes. She said goodbye and went back to her cleaning cart.

She could hear the two men continuing their banter. She felt like a bird that was just let out of a cage. There was a whole world of open air to fly in, endless horizons, but dangers too.

Annie moved her cleaning cart down the hall to her next room, a parlor suite on the west wing.

"House cleaning," Annie knocked on the door and used her passkey to let herself in. The room was perfect. It hardly looked like it was used. The bed was made with all the sheets tight as if they were not slept in. She had to strip it anyway and change the sheets, it was on her list.

When she went into the bath she saw that the room was occupied and a shaving kit was neatly arranged on the bathroom vanity. It was a very fancy leather case, with a shaving brush, a comb, and the newest kind of shaving razor with two edges. The case was open,

Annie began the routine that was required: wipe every surface, clean the toilet, the mirror, change all the sheets and pillows, straighten everything up, fold the guest's clothes...

This is odd, she thought, as she noticed the roman eagle embossed on a silver money clip.

She heard a knock on the already open door.

"Baron, it's Carla. Are you here?"

Annie showed herself and said "There's no one here."

"Oh, hello," said Carla. "I'm the baron's friend. I just need to pick up a few things."

Annie nodded. This was not her business or concern. She was just a maid. She was told to be courteous to the guests at all times and minimize contact, to be seen, but not heard.

She couldn't help but notice this woman though. She was dressed in the latest fashion: a very tight, soft-blue sweater that accented her shapely figure, a white silk blouse, a tight, navy skirt that came to her knees, nylon stockings. This was a big city girl.

Carla began to carefully go through the dresser looking for something.

"I know I left it here somewhere…" she said for Annie's benefit. "Did you see the baron?" She questioned Annie.

Annie just shook her head "no" and pretended to be mute.

As the woman bent down to explore the lower drawers, a shiny bracelet slid out from her white-silk shirt cuff. It was loaded with diamonds.

Annie broke the cardinal rule of housekeeping, and before she knew it, she blurted out: "Nice tennis bracelet!" As soon as she said it, she knew she had made a mistake.

Carla's head about snapped as she turned to look Annie square in the eyes with a "how dare you" kind of expression.

"I'm sorry, Ma'am." Annie said "I just love diamonds."

Carla's face softened as she looked down at her trophy. "I do too," she sighed. "They're not cheap."

If she only knew, thought Carla.

"He's probably gone skiing with Averell." Carla was conversing now with the housemaid.

"It's a good day for it." Annie responded like they were old pals.

If the floor boss found out she was fraternizing with guests, she would be reprimanded. But this was not the case, she was really girl-talking with a burglar.

The two had more in common than they knew. Carla was not nearly as refined as Annie, but in their present outfits, no one would know.

"Have a nice day." Carla didn't find anything, and it struck Annie, there was no sign of a woman ever being in this room. Maids mind their own, but can usually put two and two together. It helps them break the monotony of their day. Averell? Did she mean Averell Harriman, her boss, the big boss? And Baron… Wonder what that was about.

Almost done, pillow cases and cover. Nice diamonds. Annie bet they cost 1,000.00 dollars. That was some gift, she thought, not the kind of thing a young woman goes and buys for herself.

Okay, Sherlock, mind your own. She tucked the bed up, gave room 246 a once-over and locked the door.

Chapter Twenty-One

Averell Harriman and the baron met for breakfast in the Lodge dining room. Then they were driven over to the bottom of Bald Mountain, just a few miles away.

There was a big, yellow Caterpillar sitting there, already running, with a one-inch rope about 200 feet long, tied to the rear pull bar. The rope was knotted about every 20 feet.

There was construction equipment to the left of a large clearing and a big, green bullwheel on a massive cement base.

"We will have this up and running next year," said Averell, having to talk over the big Cat. "We have all the trails cleared and some of our towers up. We will have this finished next summer."

"The baron was visibly interested. In his home town, they rode cog trains up the mountains, often running through long tunnels cut through the mountains. The trains were very comfortable and slowly crawled up the Alpine hills, belching smoke from their boilers.

This was very different, a single chair, attached to a moving cable that will whisk a skier about the trees, like flying right up the hill. Not today. Today they would have to hang on to a rope for almost an hour.

Three more men showed up: Cornelius Kelley, the copper king, an experienced skier, Bunny, and Zep, the director of the ski school.

"Good morring," said the Austrian.

The baron recognized the accent as Tyrolean right away. He grew up competing against young men from this area of the Alps that ran along the borders of Italy. He didn't say a word.

"We will stop about every twenty minutes," said Averell. "Take a short rest and then break at a little lodge I've built up there."

Ted, the Cat operator, went up there yesterday and plowed the path so his machine could rumble up, knowing full well that his boss had some big shots in town. Everyone was on notice, even Zep, that this was important. Next year they would open this mountain to the world and they wanted nothing but good press.

"No problem, Mr. Harriman." Ted gave a thumbs-up sign and idled up the big machine, the warm air from the diesel engine blew onto his legs through the canvas cover that was attached to the motor shrouding.

The Cat crawled slowly forward as the men found a piece of the rope, Averell first, then the baron, then Mr. Kelley, Bunny and the ski instructor. All were strong, expert skiers.

The machine picked up speed and the clanking of the steel track became a steady beat. The Caterpillar trail was plowed down to just a few inches of snow the day before. Ted had to fight his way up the hill pushing back the drifts and deep snow as he ascended the big hill.

Then he had gone into the unfinished Round House Lodge and unloaded a large, metal box with a gallon of water, some bread, cheese, dried sausage, and two bottles of red wine. Then he built a big fire in the huge, stone fireplace and stacked some wood inside near it to dry out.

On the trip down, he set the blade just right to make a few inches of smooth base for today's trip. Mother Nature had added a dusting of new snow to clean it all up and the weather too was obliging.

As the crawler made its first turn and switched-back, the view was terrific, just blue sky, white hills with green on the north sides of the hill, across the valley.

They took two breaks on the way up to the Round House. Everyone was doing fine. The grip of the big rope was somewhat stressful, but nobody in this group would admit it or show the slightest weakness.

When they got to the Round House it was about ten in the morning. The sun was bright enough to burn your lips off. The air was still and the temperature was about 25 degrees. Perfect.

The ski instructor quickly assumed his position as guide and built the fire to a roar. The four older men warmed themselves and chatted as Zep opened the food box.

This was a routine that Averell had performed several times already this year and would several more.

"We will have another chairlift that will go from here to the very top." He pointed toward the summit. "We can't keep the trail open to the top right now, there's just too much snow." He seemed apologetic. He was like another person up here. No office protocol.

Sometimes he wished he could just leave New York behind, but that was where the money was and this place, his dream, sucked up more and more money at every turn.

"We are working with a company that's building a light-tracked machine that will ride on the snow. We hope to have the first ones here by next season."

"Service," said Zep.

And the men all sat down at a picnic table behind a big, glass-window wall, the sun beating down on a basket of bread and plates of cheese and meat.

"Here's to Averell's new chairlift." Mr. Kelley said, raising a glass of red wine.

"Here, here," said the Austrian.

"Heil Hitler," said the baron. It just blurted out before he he knew it.

There was a five-second silence then Averell said, "Well, this cheese looks good. I could eat a horse."

Mr. Kelley broke the ice. "So Averell, who is going to string this cable? That should be a challenge. I'd like to see it."

Mr. Kelley was a pit miner. Copper mines don't mess around with tunnels or cables or headframes, they just move the mountain.

"We have a local mining company here that has several cable cars and some of their men will help. Then Ted here…" Averell motioned to the Cat driver, who was just coming in from his machine and heading over to the fire. "You think we can pull a couple of miles of cable up this mountain, Ted?"

"You bet." Ted always had a can-do smile and was as ready for any challenge. "Will do 'er." He was rubbing his hands near the fire now.

He had the face of a man that spent most of his time outside. In the summer, he and his Indian wife ran a little ranch, with just thirty or forty head. They had one son and another on the way. He was a horseman and oversaw not only the big crawler, but the harness operation at the stables. There were four, large horse-teams that pulled beautiful sleds that the guests loved. The harnesses had bells that would jingle with the team's gait all through the valley.

Chapter Twenty-Two

Carla decided to take a walk in the fresh air and changed out of her city clothes into something more appropriate for the mountains. She put on a fitted pair of woolen pants lined with cotton, cut short above the boot and buttoned. She had a matching jacket with a tight sweater.

As usual, she looked fabulous, but she needed gloves, so she headed over to the ski shop and found a pair that matched with a scarf. She put it all on Averell's company account, as usual, and was walking back toward the Lodge when a beautiful team of white draft horses pulled up.

The bellman at the hotel door swung the great double doors open and the Broadway bunch piled out, talking and laughing.

Harry and Mack were kibitzing as always. They had run into Marjory Goodspeed in the lobby. Bunny was up on his skiing adventure with Averell and the baron, leaving poor, little Marjory to find her own adventure for today.

Marjory was dressed to the nines in a red, plaid Pendleton suit with fur boots. The guys all wore long wool city coats.

"Come on aboard," Mack waved Carla on.

What the hell, she thought, this was the New York bunch she flew out with.

"Why not?" She said as Mack gave her a lift up. These guys were more comfortable around attractive women than most men. They were used to being surrounded by Broadway dancers and showgirls that were always ready for a good time.

As pretty as Carla was, she was always on the defensive, she had been her whole life. Once she figured out that she was a commodity, she learned how to control her market, so to speak. But with these guys, and Marjory, who was an up-and-coming starlet, she felt like she could let her guard down a little.

"All aboard," said Harry, "train's leavin' the station."

The harness man flicked the reins and the sled moved forward, with the bells and hooves all beating in unison. A general mood of laughter and song prevailed that followed these guys wherever they went.

The sled rambled up a trail that was well-packed from numerous trips. They moved through the grand fairways of the golf course that was blanketed with a foot of snow, then along Trail Creek, upstream to a large, log cabin that was a restaurant.

The sled pulled up in front and the Maitre d' came to the door to greet them. The whole trip took about twenty minutes.

This place was like a fairy tale, Marjory thought. She remembered growing up in Buhl. Her father scratched a living with a team of six draft horses, pulling a potato harvesting wagon. She remembered living on potatoes and rabbits at times as a little girl, the dust and dirt of the Idaho farm towns with nothing for a little girl to do, but dream of getting out.

Some of her childhood friends probably have five kids by now and are struggling to feed them just like her Ma did.

She made the right decision to leave Idaho. Look where I'm at, she thought, attendants are swinging doors for me, spending her afternoon with famous Broadway producers. I've arrived. I'm living…

Truth be told, the whole bunch were running away from the lives their parents lived.

Harry's parents fled Italy because of the political oppression exerted by the Socialist Republic Party of Florence, which was seizing the wealth of the successful Catholics, who the socialists believe had abused their social positions for over two hundred years. It was payback time and because of this push, many middle class Italians fled for a new life in New York.

Mack Gordon, born Morris Gittler, fled Warsaw where Jews were being targeted. His father could see the writing on the wall, passed through the gates of Ellis Island in 1904, and settled in Brooklyn.

Mack began as a clown on the Vaudeville stages then became a comedy writer. Thus, the constant banter of Vaudeville schtick between the two writers, always laughing, telling little one-liners that you might expect to hear at a follies, innocent, but slightly off-color.

Margie laughed at everything Mack had to offer. He was a heavy man, he drank a lot and had a huge cigar in his mouth always, his hands were everywhere on Margie and she just laughed.

"Get us another drink," said Mack. "Waiter, give me a Bourbon and water on the rocks. What do you want, doll?" He had a big voice, a Broadway voice that could be heard anywhere in the room. But the room was empty, except for the staff.

"Give us two Manhattans," said Harry, pairing himself with Carla in as casual a manner as possible.

The waiters brought drinks and menus and the group began to tell New York stories.

"You know, I went sleigh riding in Central Park one time," said Mack, "yeah, I stuck my tongue on the sled and I couldn't get it off." Mack laid it up and Harry took the shot.

"You're always trying to put your tongue where it doesn't belong." Harry never missed the beat, rim shot, with his big gold ring right on the table, like they were on stage. These guys were always on stage, every minute of every day.

After several more drinks the banter shifted to musical sentencing.

"Come along take a ride on a sleigh." Harry started it off with a kind of marching beat.

"If things go well, we're gonna get laid."

"Mack, you have a one track mind," said Margie. She batted her eyes like an actress in an old, silent movie and shrugged her shoulders.

"I'm on your track, doll." He grabbed her knee.

Carla was getting in the spirit of it all. She seldom laughed this much. Most of the men that try to court her, always want to impress her with money.

The waiter brought the tray and set the steaming plate down at the table. Both the women had soup and salad. Both the men had steak. As Carla reached to the center of the table for the salt shaker, her diamonds took center stage and danced.

"Wow!" said Margie. "The Tiffany's six carat." She knew her diamonds. "You must've played a lot of tennis to get that." She was being a little rude, but by now they had consumed two drinks each and they were all loosening up. "I could learn to play tennis." She looked at Mack, who quickly took the bait.

"Margie, you're a dancer, you need to accessorize your legs." Mack could always tell a dancer. "What you need is an ankle bracelet with a little heart." He slipped his hand down passed her knee.

After lunch, they had shots of warm brandy and then called up the sled. They proceeded back towards the big lodge. The horses were moving a little faster on the return, they knew they would be going to the barn after the passengers were dropped off, and the sleigh master had to rein them back.

The air blew colder and the couples huddled under the big wool blankets that were provided on the sled.

Mack and Margie began to kiss, but the ride was too bumpy and they just gave up. Carla was already mildly attracted to this man, but in a most superficial way.

Mack reached up and tapped the driver on the shoulder and waved a one dollar bill at him. "Driver, bring us around the backside of the hotel and let us out at the pool."

Chapter Twenty-Three

"Follow me," said Averell, and he pushed off with the enthusiasm of a schoolboy. Bunny followed, then Mr. Kelley. The baron waited to be last, but Zep was going to run "sweep". In case anyone in the party fell, he could assist them.

The baron understood that, but did not want an Austrian behind him, so the two men waited on a top of the big hill, in an awkward silence that you could cut with a knife, more like a sword.

Zep hated everything this guy stood for. He was receiving news from family members in the old country, books and magazines too.

Six months ago, he was sent a manifesto printed by Hitler, about sixty pages that clearly outlined what was going to be Hitler's plan to purge Germany, Austria, and Poland of all but the strongest of the old German families.

Many of the remote, little mountain villages in Alps had large percentages of inbreeding from years of seclusion. In some cases, first cousins had married to keep land or businesses in the family. This often resulted in children with birth defects, retardation or epilepsy.

Germany's social programs, which were initiated by Baron von Bismarck, could not handle the increase of people dependent on the government. The German banks were printing more and more paper money and it was buying less and less. The healthier, working population of small businesses, many who were Jews, were being forced to pick up the tab. Government offices were extracting taxes and fines from the middle class and Hitler seized on this, creating an army of supporters that were nothing more than an angry mob in tailored-woolen suits and big, black boots. And the most frightening concept for anyone with half a brain was the talk of "Total War". That was the bright idea of putting every man woman and child in the service of a military hell-bent on conquering neighboring countries.

"You go," said the baron, in the most proper of German dialects, notifying Zep of his station.

Zep responded in the most rural of Tyrolean hill-dialects: "I don't want to be hit from behind by a wild pig."

This was going to be a race down. No other way.

This was Zep's mountain. He was the guide, he was the pro, and he wasn't going to let a Nazi from Garmisch tell him what to do.

The two men, who both grew up racing, pushed off at the same time. The rest of the party was long gone around a turn and could not be seen from above. Averell had pulled up and the others stopped alongside him.

"How was that?" Averell was one big smile.

"Great," said Bunny.

"Where are they?" Mr. Kelley was looking up the hill, but the trail had a long, broad curve and that thick pine forest blocked the view uphill.

The mountain was deafly silent, the air was still. It was about 20 degrees and super sunny.

The men could hear a sound like an air leak in a hose, or leaves rustling, as the two competitors came flying around the curve in a full-tucked position. They were going over 50 miles an hour.

As they streaked by, Averell could hear little phrases in German dialects, mingled with grunts and groans.

"That is suicide." Averell said to Kelley.

"I've never seen anybody go that fast." Mr. Kelley was tracking them like a setter on point.

"I hope they know what they're doing," said Bunny. "I would hate to send the baron home in a cast."

"Or a pine box," said Averell. "We have a lot of money on the line here."

Averell was both angry and proud of his ski school director. If the baron was hurt, it could be bad for business. If he lost the race, he would be in a bad mood for the rest of the trip.

None of this was going through the minds of the two men barreling down the mountain. Winning this was all they each cared about, far more than the Americans could possibly grasp. The baron realized early on that Zep had the advantage: the Austrian was in his own equipment, it was broken in, he had probably waxed his own skies that past evening, and bragged to his buddies in the ski school shed that he was going to the big mountain they were calling Baldy. He had oil-soaped his boots too.

The baron was in new equipment from the rental shop. The boots were stiff and hard. The leather tops cut into his ankle like a medieval torture rack. He controlled his pain. The cold air flooded his face, as the powder from Zep's tail stung his eyes.

Zep had on thick, high-altitude climbing glasses with leather blinders. They were fogging up some, so he couldn't see any better than the baron.

Both men's hearts were pounding like pile drivers, the rush was a combination of anger, pride, macho, and an insatiable need for speed.

The baron knew the snow would be colder along the tree line on the shaded side of the slope and he had to break out of the wind tunnel of Zeppie. Control, stay low, legs apart, so the air can move through, breathe… He thought to himself.

Zep couldn't even tell were the baron was. He could be splatted up against a big Doug-fir, for all he knew.

Then the baron appeared in the right side of his ice-covered glasses. He's in the colder snow, Zep could push him into the trees, he thought. The Austrian was seething with anger and adrenaline.

Zep realized as soon as he saw him, the snow would be colder, so it would be faster, but Zep was waxed, and the difference for him would be immeasurable.

Their legs were on fire by now, their muscles straining from the pressure of a prolonged-tuck position. No surrender now. They were both hot and cold, exhausted and exhilarated, about another mile to go. Hang on.

The rest of the party was tailing them at a safer and more reasonable pace. Everyone was watching the dust trails, neck and neck. This is more exhilarating than the Belmont, thought Averell.

As the two racers approached the last, long gentle grade to the bottom, they were at a dead-tie, the baron hugging the tree line in the shade, Zep tracking in the sun, counting on his wax to make up the difference. He couldn't cut to the right, that would be cheating, not an option. The honor of his homeland was at stake here.

The baron was a good competitor, thought Zep. He was ten years older, and a few inches taller, this gave Zep another slight edge, but the cold snow along the tree line was a good choice and the two men crossed the imaginary finish line together, doing all they could to pull up and not go right into the river.

As they came to a screeching halt, they were both breathing so hard they couldn't say a word if they wanted to. They said nothing, just a flash of a stare, as if to say: I'm better than you. No, you're not. You're not worth my respect, but damn, that was fun.

For five heart-pounding minutes, they were boys, back in the Alps, before the world had gone mad, before the little shops in the village that made the pastries and chocolates they loved were marked and smashed by the mobs, before the Fatherland turned on its own children.

Chapter Twenty-Four

Mack lay flat on his back on the pool lounger. He was wearing nothing but a terry cloth hotel robe and a latex condom. Margie was screwing him with a vengeance.

"Ride 'em, cowgirl." Mack growled.

They had drunk about six drinks by now and had a big dinner. He, as always, was still smoking a fat cigar and cracking jokes. Margie felt like she was fucking a bull walrus. Steam was coming off them both. It was broad daylight and hardly appropriate behavior for midday in a hotel pool, but almost everyone was on Dollar Mountain skiing and wouldn't think about coming back until after 3:00 p.m.

They didn't care anyway, they were both tanked. He was horny and she was going to screw her way into this picture, a bad decision on her part because if Bunny found out, not only would she get fired from the Union Bank job, but she probably would get tossed out on her ear and end up back in Buhl --via bus from Sun Valley.

They were still going at it when Harry made his move on Carla and took her by the hand towards the men's locker room. They both still had their pants on and they had been sunning themselves poolside as far away from Mack and Margie as possible, not quite as randy, or at least Carla wasn't.

She had her turtleneck pulled up so just her belly was getting sun. She was driving Harry wild and enjoyed that.

She followed when he took her by the hand and the two were walking into the men's lockers when a man came out suddenly.

"Carla? Carla Green?" said the man in a kind of Idaho farm accent. "I'm your cousin, Arthur. Mr Shoup, from *The Record* told me you would be here."

She had never seen this guy in her life.

"Oh, Carla." He said, as he hugged her while Harry was still holding her hand. "It's been years, since Christmas at Uncle Shoup's."

Harry was about to get laid and had a tent in his trousers that you could see from down the hall, but this guy was messing with his program. Carla was worked up too and ready to go with it. She was drunk, but not to a stupor, and the words *Uncle Shoup* triggered a clearing in the clouds that were up in her pretty, little, horny head.

"Oh? Cousin Arthur…" she said, slowly at first, then, as she snapped out of it a little, she began to see he was here to save her ass from herself. "Great to see you. How are you?"

Harry let go of her hand, his plans dashed.

"Excuse me," he said, "I've …" and he pointed to the john. "You know…" And he went into the men's locker room.

"Are you nuts?" whispered the man, dropping the phony cowboy accent and reverting to his natural Austrian-American tongue. "If you stray from our plan, we could all get killed or at least, our families back home. You have got to stay focused. Get your clothes. We've got to get you out of here, this hotel has eyes."

"Cousin Arthur" had been keeping tabs on Carla and the baron from the first day they arrived. He was in contact with the waiters at the cabin where they had lunch. He saw them in the

108

pool the first night. His job was to make sure that Baron von Tippelskirch did not leave Idaho--ever. In fact, he planned to leave the body for the wolves.

Carla grabbed her wool jacket, tucked her shirt back in, and stumbled some as she let her "cousin" take her by the arm up the hallway towards the hotel restaurant.

"We've got to get some coffee in you," he said.

As they headed up the hall from the pool to the lobby, Harry came out of the locker room.

"Honey, where are you going?" He said in a pleading, pathetic cry.

"I'll see you later, Harry." She waved, but didn't turn around as she walked off. "Thanks for lunch."

Chapter Twenty-Five

The baron and Zep continued to ignore each other as the bus pulled up in front of the Lodge lobby. The men piled out, sun-burned faces, jackets opened and tired from their adventure.

"Let's get a beer," said Averell. "Who wants a beer?"

"I do," said Bunny.

"Me, too," said Mr. Kelley.

They headed toward the bar.

Zep just fell out of formation without a comment. His task was done and he needed time to recover from the anger that boiled up inside of him. The man that he had just broken bread with was part of the invading army that took over his homeland, an army that was groomed from youth to feel superior to all others, to the extent that they were prepared to enslave their neighboring countries, just like Rome did.

In fact, Hitler loved everything about ancient Rome and its system of conquest that ruled Europe for a thousand years. He even took the Roman salute for his own. He expected nothing less of his plan for Europe, and if the baron could come home with this purchase of aircraft fuel and TEL, the Luftwaffe could take all of Europe in one, huge blitzkrieg.

It had to, because Germany did not have the fuel to last any more than one shot. It would be the biggest military gamble in history, the best steel guns, some so large that locomotives toiled to haul them down heavy tracks. They had the steel alright, the hardest of metals, but they lacked the softest of metals: lead.

Chapter Twenty-Six

Rupert was very pleased with the production at "the Strike". This year his mine was going to be one of the largest producers in Idaho and possibly number one. The North Star Mine produced 4,000 ounces of gold--off some from years prior, 1,549,000 ounces of silver, 14,069,000 pounds of lead--the most ever and a peak production that would decline in years to come until closing. The mine also produced a record breaking 22,920,000 pounds of zinc. The US Navy would need every bit and then some in the next three years.

This was a production level that the men could all be proud of, up almost 100% from the previous year. It made the Triumph the number two mine in Idaho, by a very slim margin.

Most of the lead was destined for Tetraethylene lead production. The zinc went for ships. The silver was used for what would become known shortly in following years as "electronics". And the gold was not really in demand for much. World currencies were in a mess. Weddings, a large source of gold use, were down. Couples were too poor to get married and raise a family. Morals were loose. Alcoholism was up. We were a country in limbo, waiting for the next shoe to drop.

In 1938, the Boston Naval Shipyard built two ships, both destroyers. By 1944, they would be building fifty large ships a year. The amount of raw materials needed for the construction of war equipment was about to become daunting.

Not much of this was of concern to Rupe, he was just a miner and a family man: Show up, do your job, don't get hurt, and go home to your family. He made almost eight dollars a day, very high pay at a time when unemployment was nearing 30%.

"Are you skiing after your shift, Romeo?" He questioned Rowdey as the late night came to a close and men were preparing for the blast.

"Not today, boss," said Rowdey. "I'm going into Sun Valley to meet Annie. She's getting me a pass and we're going skiing on the chairlift." He was focusing his attention on stowing his tools and equipment in his locker in the North Star bunkhouse, when the blast went off and everything around them shook like a freight car. Little puffs of dust fell from the cracks in the plaster ceilings.

"Well, there she blows," said Rupe. "Be careful. I'll see you tomorrow. When are you going to make an honest woman out of that girl?" He said as Rowdey put on his heavy winter coat.

"I wish I could, but she's going back east to become a professor in the spring. See ya, boss." He headed down the hill, to his truck.

"Professor, huh? That's good work if you can get it… Have fun." Rupe hollered to a young man running to his lover.

Rowdey headed for the Sun Valley Lodge.

Chapter Twenty-Seven

Mr. Kelley and Mr. Harriman were having one of their last casual, cold beers for a long time, not a care in the world.

"You really have done a magnificent job here, Averell." Mr. Kelley sat back in a comfortable couch as the waitress brought them each a bottle of beer.

"Thanks," said Averell. "I'm planning on a movie production to bring it to the public." He sat back and stretched his legs. "I've got the writers here now, working on it."

Max and Margie had progressed to the women's shower room in the pool complex and were going at it again, this time he had her up against the wall in front of a large, mirrored, marble vanity. He had slipped the desk attendant a dollar and asked her to take a walk.

Bunny came out of the men's room, up the hall, and joined the other men in the conversation. The baron also came in and ordered a large glass of cold beer.

"We just have bottles," said the bartender, and he uncapped an ice cold Budweiser.

The men all drank and enjoyed the comfort of the hotel bar. An hour ago, they were on a giant mountain, skiing down in the fresh air. This was as good as it gets.

"Well, Baron…" Averell started the conversation, "What do you think of my little mountain?"

The baron took a long, cold drink of beer. "Ah," he quenched his thirst. "It's fantastic. The mountains here are very special. The air is so dry and so clean." He wasn't just being nice. "The slopes are so even, not like my country. The snow is drier, very interesting. I would highly recommend this place to anyone."

Averell was soaking it up. This was the same assessment on the conditions that his people had made. The high desert is very different than the Alps and unless you spent time in both places, it would be hard to explain, but damp cold air like Vermont or Zermatt cuts through your clothes, freezes on the skin, causes frostbite. The dry desert air has none of those negative winter effects and at this altitude, sunburn is more of a problem than frostbite.

"Averell," Mr. Kelley changed the subject. "How would you rate Roosevelt's policies so far?"

"They're killing me," said Averell, in a kidding kind of manner. "The import-export restrictions on metals and raw materials, the seizure of all gold… We have a gold, silver operation right on the other side of that hill." He raised his bottle and pointed to the Triumph, that sits a mile to the south of the Lodge bar.

"Oh, really," said the baron. "I would like to see that. My mother was from Salzburg and I was down in the salt mines many times as a boy." He suddenly showed an interest. "Could we go see this gold mine?"

"Actually," said Averell, "It's a galena mine. Galena is an ore that contains silver, lead, zinc, gold, iron pyrite and iridium, in varying degrees."

"Don't forget copper," said Mr. Kelley, the copper king.

"Much of the lead you are purchasing comes from here, goes to Utah, to Mr. Kelley's town, and then gets shipped to New Jersey for processing into TEL."

All of a sudden, the men were talking shop.

"Raw materials are what make the world go round," toasted Mr. Kelley.

"Yes, but love happens on the spin," said Averell.

"To love," said Bunny.

"To love," said the baron.

The men enjoyed their beers and then Mr. Kelley got up and said, "Averell, thank you for a wonderful day." He was getting his things together. "Glad to meet you. You're a very good skier. Gentlemen, I'm going to take a little nap." And he retired to his room.

"That sounds like a plan," said Averell. "Can we all meet back here for dinner at seven?"

"Yes. I could use a rest," said the baron. The two men shook hands. "Thank you for a wonderful day. You have a fantastic mountain. I would like to see this galena mine if I could."

"We can go tomorrow," said Averell. "I will make the arrangements."

Averell nodded to Bunny to do so and he returned the nod.

The baron bowed ever so slightly to his new friends and headed for the elevator. Averell tipped the bartender, thanked the bar staff for a job well done, and left for the comfort of his suite.

The baron got off the elevator on the third floor and walked down the hall toward Carla's room. He was hoping for at least a back rub. He knocked on her door.

"Who is it?" Carla said. "Just a minute."

She came to the door with her hair up in a white towel, wearing a hotel robe.

As soon as he saw her he became aroused. She was beautiful and mysterious. To his surprise, she put her two arms on his shoulders, letting go of her robe and allowing it to open, exposing her beautiful body.

"Are you ready for another massage?" She said, gently pulling him in from the hallway.

"Could you scratch my back?"

She said, "Ya, of course."

He felt lucky. This was turning into a day to remember. He closed the door behind him, reaching inside her open robe and grabbing her waist, pulling her to him, they fell on the bed.

Chapter Twenty-Eight

Rowdey was setting his rock drill for a shift. They had reached an area in the Plummer Winze that had unusual gold content compared to the rest of the ore body. Production was continuing to climb and the company received an additional Defense Minerals Exploration contract.

It was becoming clearer to the boys in Washington that war was inevitable and strategic metals would be needed in huge amounts.

Rowdey didn't spend much time thinking about the workings of Washington. He had to stay totally focused on the task at hand or somebody might get hurt. He kidded around on the ride in and out of "the Strike", but once he was on the job, it was a team effort and safety was everything. He was working with Wes, a new man up from California. They had been drilling down on the 800-foot level into the Annie #54, looking for new veins. The plan was to go 500 feet straight west, in the hope of hitting the same type of formation that was in the Plummer tunnel at the North Star.

At the 800-foot level, the geology changed some and they began to see small pockets of river sand with sea shells. This change had them both a little on edge and they were extra careful. The air was different and the company was concerned about gases, or lack of oxygen that could dull a man's senses.

About a month earlier, in the Triumph shaft elevator, a worker got into the elevator and laid a piece of drill steel across the ore cart that he was sharing the space with. When the cable pulled the elevator up, the drill steel caught on part of the shaft blocking and flung the drill steel, killing the man instantly.

State inspectors showed up and laid the blame on the worker, but things were still tense and the company ramped up safety efforts.

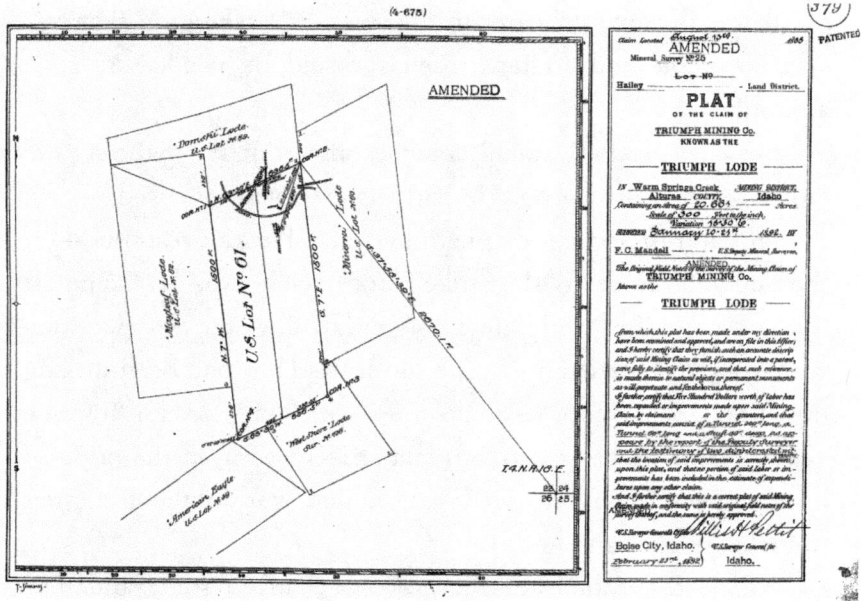

The two men continued to drill the set of holes to move their tunnel forward. As they approached the end of the shift, they set up the rock drill for one more hole. They had repeated this task seven times already on the shift. Rowdey set the steel tripod with the screw set and Wes lifted the rock drill up on the stand. It weighed close to 100 pounds and Wes strained to put it atop the tripod. Rowdey used his free hand to assist and the tool was attached to the stand.

Wes picked up the air lines and attached the air hose to the back of the rock drill with a twist. At the same time, Rowdey was installing the six-foot drill steel.

Once all the parts were connected, they turned on the air and the drill began to rattle. The men turned the heavy iron wheel that pushed the drill steel into the rock face. The drill steel had a small hole that ran inside of it that allowed air to pass through, blowing the rock dust clear of the hole as the bit gnawed its way into the mountain.

Dust usually was expelled from the drill, but Rowdey noticed that a damp, grey paste was drooling down from the hole. This meant they were into wet rock.

The paste could jam the drill tool and bind it up, making their job much harder. The experienced miners slowed down on the feed and let the drill work its way into this last hole of their shift. When the drill bit was into the whole the full-length of the rod, almost six feet, they stopped the machine and reversed it out.

"Easy," barked Rowdey. "I don't want to spend another hour digging this drill steel out, don't let it bind."

"I got it," said Wes. He turned on the air to the little hole in the drill steel to blow out the sludge in the hole and it blew a spray of the grey muck on them both.

"Shit," said Rowdey. "This is a damn wet hole. There must be a ground water pocket here." He was wiping the nasty mud of his face and lips. "Taste sweet," he said, "like pancakes."

"Don't remind me, I'm hungry."

They laughed, but couldn't work the drill steel out of the hole. The soupy sludge turned to cement as the heat from the friction cooked the mess together.

The two men struggled for twenty minutes when Rupert showed up on his rounds. He always liked to check to the crews that were hunting more ore.

Once a body of ore was found, the muckers would scoop it out of the mountain, but finding it, that was the challenge, reading the geology, that's how it was done, from years of experience.

"You can't tell where you're going, if you don't know where you've been," he used to say.

"What do we got?" The boss always seemed to show up at the wrong time.

"We're stuck, boss" said Rowdey. "It was a wet hole and then we got bound up. You want us to just leave the steel and move on?"

"Let's see," Rupert said. "Get the powder and caps. I'll get the drill out."

He disconnected the rod from the drill, unscrewed the big toggles that held the drill on the stand and lifted it off and set it on the ore cart behind them like it was nothing. At 40, he was still stronger than most of the men in the hill.

"Get me a sledge and a pipe wrench from the work box," he barked. "You guys were rushing on your last hole, feeding too fast, look where it got ya."

He pounded on the end of the steel with the big mallet and then reached for the pipe wrench.

"Grab the sledge and tap it, not hard." He motioned to Rowdey as he worked the drill steel counter clockwise. It was barely moving

"There," he said. "Hook it all back up. It'll come out now." He was confident in his assessment

The two younger men did as they were told and when the air was let back into the tool the steel drill spun itself out of the rockface followed by a stream of soupy grey sluge.

They unscrewed the jack stand and set it with the drill on the cart. Everything was covered with the grey paste and they were a mess.

"Go on, wrap it up," said the boss. "Let's get out of here."

"I'm going to hit the showers," said Rowdey.

"Me too," said Wes.

Rowdey had several pieces of fuse cut into 10-foot lengths and was using a special crimping tool that attached a blasting cap to the fuse. Then Wes took a wooden dowel that was sharpened to a stake, like a pencil, and poked a small hole into the dynamite. He carefully inserted the copper cap with the fuse crimped onto it.

Rowdey passed him a broom stick and he carefully pushed the dynamite to the back of the hole.

"Packing," he called.

"Here ya go, buddy." Rowdey pulled strips of pre-cut rags from a bag on the little work cart.

Wes shoved it in the hole and tamped it tight, keeping the fuse on the bottom of the drill hole.

"That hole keeps running," he said, "that's different." Curious, he thought, must be a big water pocket.

They finished setting the fuse and tied the eight pieces of fuse together in a manner so one 10-foot piece of slow fuse could be attached. Fuses were rated at different burns times, allowing the miners to make safe exits.

At half past six, they had stashed the little work wagon with all the tools and supplies about 50 yards back from their work area. Then Rowdey found a dry rag in the box and wiped his hands so he could strike a match and light the fuse. They had done this so many times that it all worked like a well-oiled machine.

The fuse was lit, They hooked up the air to the automatic mucking machine, charged the tank and pushed the ore cart down the tunnel and headed out, covered with grey mud, lamps still bright, shining a beam of light in the tunnel leading them to the surface, lunch pails in hand.

"That was a bear," said Wes.

"Yea," said Rowdey. "It's not always easy."

At 7:00 a.m., their charges went off along with all the others set at various locations in the tunnel system. The whole mountain shook as the crews were already at the North Star bunkhouse grabbing cups of hot coffee and biscuits that the company cook had waiting for the hungry workers.

As the men sat and swapped comments, the rock faces at the collective blast sites all crumbled, forcing the mountain to yield to the workers.

But at the 800-foot level, a wall of water broke through, unleashing a flood that filled the lower tunnels in minutes with millions of gallons of water.

Had the two men been there, they would have drowned. Little did they know, as they skied down, off the hill that morning, carving turns in the fresh snow without a care in the world, they had cheated death.

They would not hear about the flood until the next day. Production would be curtailed for a month as the company scrambled to add pumps and increase power and air lines to run them.

In spite of the flood and setbacks, the Triumph still had its biggest year and ended up the number two producer in the state and the number three in the US.

It was a good thing because the country was headed to war with Germany and the military buildup would be more than anyone could have foreseen.

Chapter Twenty-Nine

It was another sunny day, white, blue, and green, the color palette of the Idaho winter.

Averell's driver met the four men in front of the Lodge at 8:00 a.m. Bunny had called Mr. Swent at the Triumph office and informed him that some of the majority stockholders in the American Smelting and Refining Company (ASARCO) were coming to tour the mine along with Mr. Kelley from Anaconda Copper.

Swent hopped to, "Yes, sir, we would be honored. We did have an incident last night, sir, so if you don't mind, could we keep the visit down to a few hours?"

"What kind of incident?" said Bunny.

"We broke into what looks like an underground river and around 200 feet of our lower levels flooded last night in a few hours. We are bringing in some extra pumps today. Our main strike is on an upper level, so production is proceeding on target, sir."

The Swede wanted to make sure that Bunny understood that the production levels were maintained.

The company received government loans from Roosevelt's Recovery Act and had to follow very strict guidelines in an almost draconian fashion.

Roosevelt's financial advisors were grasping at straws trying to pull the country out of the lingering recession. They created thousands of pages of rules, regulations, and quotas --across every level of American industry.

Many thought these rules just made things worse and made government bigger. It seized all privately-owned gold except for wedding bands and crosses. This devalued gold by 40% and inflated the cost of paper money, having the reverse of the intended consequence.

In an effort to increase commodity values, the government thought that destroying wealth would create demand, so they actually destroyed crops when people were starving. Then, the government killed and buried thousands of cattle and pigs. They started the concept of a minimum wage that caused millions of poor, black farm workers to lose their jobs, because nobody could afford to buy products with inflated prices. Roosevelt's programs lost more jobs than they created.

At the Triumph, gold was a nice little sweetener to the bottom line. It was running a little less than a tenth of an ounce per ton, so its overall value added about enough to pay for the labor costs of the whole shift.

Not only did Roosevelt's action cut that in half, but the labor unions found new strength with Roosevelt's Socialist ideology and they demanded more pay.

So with the stroke of the president's pen, the government reached into ASARCO's pocket and took 25% of its profit.

It really took the whole operation, because Uncle Sam set the price, demanded that quotas were met -- or there were fines.

Jack Rutter understood what was happening. He saw Socialism take over the iron mines in northern Spain and run the country into extreme poverty, leading to the revolution that was about to explode on the world stage.

Swent walked across the yard from the Payroll Office to the company store were Jack keep his desk. "Jack," Swent grabbed Jack around his shoulders. "I need a favor."

"What's going on?" said Jack, always ready to jump.

"We have visitors coming this morning in about twenty minutes and they are kind of big shots from the East Coast. I need you to give them a tour of the mill and our operation here and then take them in the Plummer tunnel and show them "the Strike". I've explained to them that we are dealing with a flooding problem today so we had to keep it short. The road has been plowed to the North Star and you can put them all on the back of the truck. It's chained up."

Jack had been on the phone all morning with pump suppliers in Salt Lake and had already ordered three of the best pumps in stock and they were already on trucks and en route. They would arrive late in the afternoon and extra crews were scheduled to begin moving them into the lower levels.

The problem was compounded some because the pumps had to be broken down to fit in the Triumph elevator, that rickety, old 700-foot shaft that killed a man the year before. It was two feet by four feet and seven feet tall, with a piece of track on its floor so an ore car and two men could fit in it, tight.

There were many kinds of pumps available. Jack settled on an air pump that would use compressed air to move water to the 600-foot level, into tanks. Then, a pair of triplex style plunger pumps would move it from the 500-foot level to the surface.

Jack had ordered the pipe fitting shop to begin cutting and threading all the three-inch pipe they had in stock to lengths they could get into the elevator. That was the only way into the lower levels.

127

He also placed an order for more pipe and fittings, and flexible three-inch fire hose. That was already being loaded at Western Mine Supply in Salt Lake and would be out of the yard in an hour, headed north. He had only to wait, so, tour... Why not, thought Jack, what else could go wrong?

Averell, the baron, and Mr. Kelley rolled into Triumph in the Sun Valley limousine. The driver pulled up in front of the company store.

The company store consisted of one room with a little walk-up counter, Jack's desk (behind that counter), a Coca-Cola machine, some candy, and two small, metal mail baskets for outgoing mail. There was a cabinet on the wall with 40 pigeon holes for mail and every day the mail was delivered from Hailey.

The mail lady supplemented her income by selling eggs and milk. She had a small chicken coop in town and just carried the milk as a service. It was the custom of the women of the village to gather and gossip on the little patio in front of the store. There were several that morning, chattering about babies and dinners. The long, black Cadillac would be a topic of their speculation for several days.

One woman, who was married to the local preacher, commented in a whisper, "Look how they flaunt their money." She said, "The bible says that the meek shall inherit the earth."

"I'm still waiting..." said another.

"Ladies," Averell tipped his hat to them like they were local dignitaries, "lovely day."

They all smiled and then they slowly dispersed.

Averell walked into the company store and Jack greeted and shook his hand.

"I'm Jack Rutter," he said. Like most people, Averell was surprised to hear a proper English accent in the middle of the Idaho wilderness.

The baron stood out in the middle of the street and looked around like a conquering hero. He was feeling his oats this morning.

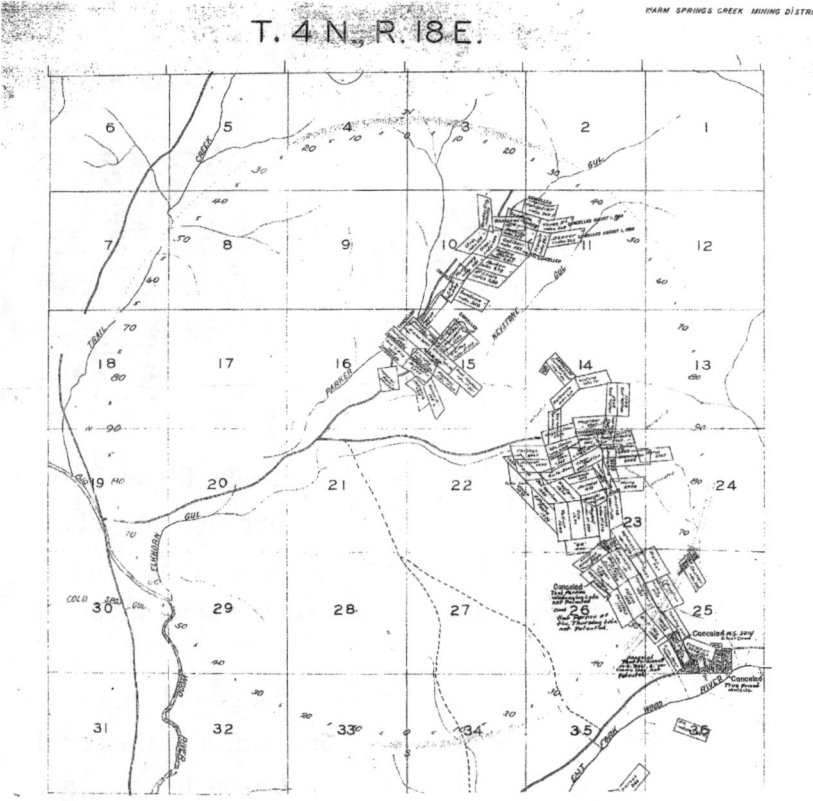

Bunny chose not to come. Margie was a little under the weather and he decided to stay with her today. The driver took the time to tinker with the big sixteen-cylinder Caddy and was wiping it down a bit. He would soon settle into reading the Hailey newspaper and watching the car. Local kids began to gather around the fancy auto. The arrival of a car like that in Triumph was not an everyday occurrence.

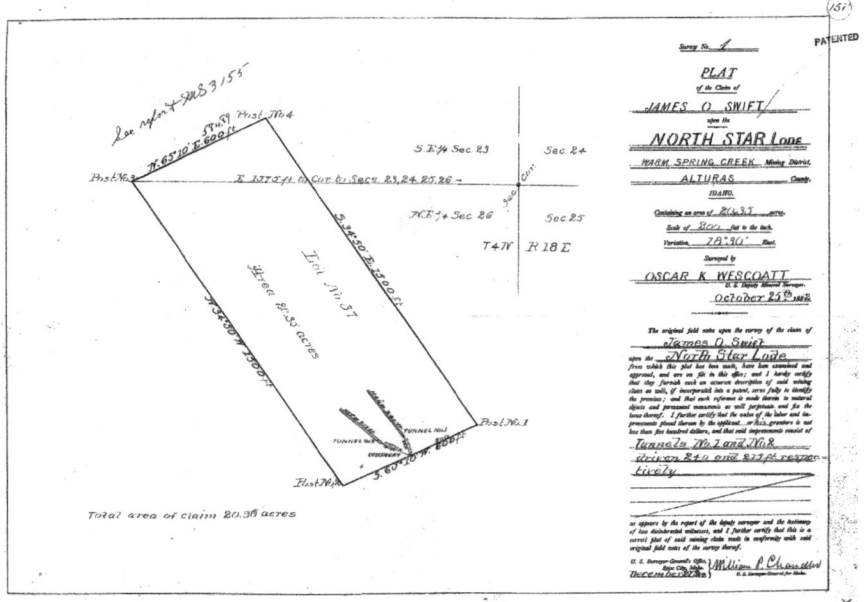

Jack was ready for his guests. Normally Rupert would conduct a tour like this, but the flood had him running full-bore this morning. Jack and he had already agreed to meet with them in the mountain, at "the Strike", which was not at all affected by the flood.

The three men were fitted with light packs and lamps. Mr. Kelley didn't need any help with the equipment, so he helped the baron plug his up. They all were given brown helmets, gray-striped coveralls and blue denim jackets. They also removed their boots and put on rubber boots. When they got suited-up, Jack checked them over and made sure all the miners' lamps were working.

"Okay, gentlemen, welcome to the Triumph Mine, my name is Jack Rutter. I'm the Surface Boss here at the Triumph. This year we are on track to be the largest producer of silver, lead and zinc in the world. It's going to be close. We will definitely be in the top three. It's a big world."

Jack looked at the baron and knew what he was without even speaking to him. The arrogance, the hair cut, the big black boots: he was German military. Why was he here?

"First we will view the stamp mill, and for that, gentlemen, I'd like to give you at these cotton balls to put in your ears. It's loud in there."

The noise from the stamp mill was easily heard from where they were standing at the store, even though baffles were installed in the upper rooms housing the stamp machines.

The stamp mill ran for a 10-hour shift. The building had an air powered whistle that blew at noon and again at six. The local women could set their watches by it. Kids knew to be home for lunch or dinner.

Smoke billowed from the boiler, as warm water was needed to run the shaker tables in winter or the whole place would freeze up. It was very clean inside, the floors were kept swept, and material that got onto the floor was swept up and put back in the circuit.

"We have six of these shaker tables," Jack explained. The three men were all familiar with this type of machinery, especially Mr. Kelley. The Anaconda had ten times as many.

The baron's attention was drawn to the white salts that built up on the wooden borders of the troughs, coming and going from the tables. He recognized it immediately as lead salt or lead acetate.

This was the main ingredient in Goulard's Extract. It was also called *sugar of lead* and had been used for centuries to sweeten wine at orgies, as it produces mild psychotropic episodes -- an effect that might liven up any party.

"Follow me," said Jack.

Averell waved his hand. It was getting very loud as they approached the stamp mill. "We don't need to see the crushers," he hollered. "We really just want to see 'the Strike'."

Jack never missed a beat. "Okay, let's get out of here."

He didn't enjoy the mill, it was too noisy. The mill was the cash machine of the operation, but it was not a place to spend a lot of time. The mill man was often seen taking a nip, and Jack somehow understood.

As the group headed back down the steps through the building, they passed through the loading bins filled with the heavy concentrate. The baron fell back some and pulled a hotel envelope and pen from his jacket pocket. He quickly collected several tablespoons of lead acetate from the wood at the bottom of the ore chutes, carefully folded the envelope and put it in his pocket.

The group had moved to the yard and waited for him to catch up.

"Let's jump on that truck, fellas, and we will run up the hill."

The company truck fired up and all three men decided to sit on the bed and enjoy the ride. It was a very mild, sunny winter day and the view was terrific as the Chevy climbed the road to the North Star Mine. They made two switchbacks and then a long gentle climb to the upper buildings. When they got to the upper ore chutes and the bunkhouse, Jack parked the truck near the old mule sheds and set the break.

"Gentlemen..." They followed and entered into the Plummer tunnel.

The warm air of the earth felt good on their skin as they followed Jack, the lights of their lamps shining a path up the tunnel.

"This is our main tunnel at this level," said Jack. "It's about a mile long and comes out the other side of the mountain at a workings and headframe that goes down 800 feet. Right now, we are scrambling down there to deal with a flood situation. Seems as though they broke into an underground lake or river and 300 feet of workings flooded yesterday in a few hours. It's under control. It will not affect our production levels. Our main working ore body is right up ahead, and we are going to break our previous production records this year," Jack assured them.

He assumed that meeting the quotas set by the terms of the National Recovery Act contract was all the company bosses cared about. There were fines imposed if a company that took the loan money did not meet contract quotas.

The quotas were not a haphazard assessment. The government's geologists did extensive studies to estimate the ore reserves in the mountain. Then a contract was issued based on those studies and an acceptable production schedule had to be met. The prices were all fixed at a national standard.

The Recovery Act set prices on over 2000 items, from minerals to vegetables and everything in between. Some economists said it was good, others argued it was terrible.

At the Triumph, it meant good jobs when people in the flatlands were hungry. There was no arguing with Uncle Sam. He set the price on the strategic metals and set the price for the labor. He also kept the price of gold low. Jack was suspect of that, but he too was glad to have a job.

As they approached "the Strike", Jack turned around announced to the men, "We are coming on to one of the largest ore faces ever developed, gentlemen. It's over 700 hundred feet long and 50 feet tall." Jack did not spend much time in here, except to make sure his timbers were delivered and the blocking was up to par.

As he turned to address the men, he noticed the baron collecting a sample of the fungus material growing on the red iron rock and damp timber sets.

"Are you planning on traveling with Homer, sir? Jack stuck his foot in his mouth and regretted it as soon as he said it. The others had no idea what the hell he was talking about, but the baron did and responded to the inside joke in kind.

"No, sir," said the baron. "I have no desire to tangle with the demons of Hellena."

The two men, both classically trained, knew exactly what they were referring to. But Averell and Mr. Kelley just focused their eyes on "the Strike".

"Like an Eleusinian mystery, so shiny, so beautiful," said Jack, staring the baron straight on.

Both Averell and Mr. Kelley had no idea what was going on between the two men, but they could tell it was not congenial. This was the second time in as many days that the baron created an uncomfortable silence.

Averell was aware of the tension and again broke it with a comment. "Jack," he smiled, "this is a wonderful and impressive ore body. We are lucky to have it and we're glad we have you."

Now he was pouring on unnecessary praise, but Jack took it.

"Thank you, sir. I'm glad to have a job."

Not quite the answer Averell expected, but it was honest and he respected that.

The two men were equals in wit, if not wealth. The main difference being, Averell had inherited 80 million bucks from his daddy.

The men concluded the tour and took the truck down the hill. They got out of the coveralls and hung them up in the shop.

As they were putting on their street shoes, Rup came in for a Coke and a visit.

"Hello," he said to Mr. Harriman, stretching his hand out for a handshake.

Jack introduced everyone.

"How's the flood repair going?" asked Mr. Kelley.

The two took an instant liking to each other. Miners were a brotherhood like no other.

"Good, we'll have it under control in a week. There's a lot of water down there, but once the pumps arrive, it won't take long to set them in place."

Rupe was as confident as could be and it showed.

"We enjoyed our visit, thank you," said Averell. "Let's get back to town."

And with that, the men loaded into the warm comfortable V-16 Cadillac and the driver rolled down East Fork.

About three miles down the road, the first of four heavy trucks was making its way up the hill, loaded down with big pumps from Salt Lake.

"Looks like your boys got things under control, Averell," said Mr. Kelley.

"Yea, I like those guys, they're good men."

Chapter Thirty

"How did the inspection go?" said Rupe.

"I think it went okay, but one of those guys is up to no good," said Jack.

"Whadaya mean?"

"The big German kept taking lead white samples and then when I saw him scrape some of the slime molds into a envelope I was sure and I called him on it."

Jack was looking down the valley as if he was seeing through time.

"I still don't know what the hell you're talking about," said Rupe.

"Did you ever read Homer?" Jack looked at Rup.

"I knew a guy named Homer once. I boxed his ears off in the Twin Falls Golden Glove championships, but I don't think he was a writer." He was clowning around.

"Homer wrote the Greek tragedies over two-thousand years ago, three-hundred years before Christ. They were tales of the adventures of a young hero. In these tales, Apollo Stands upon his head..."

"Did he wear a helmet?" said Rupe, still clowning.

"Sometimes," said Jack, "the translation from Ancient Greek is more like 'a visit from god'."

Jack seldom rattled off snippets from his formal English education. He wasn't a snob, although many of the men

136

perceived him to be so. He always wore a tweed jacket and tie because that was the dress for a *man of letters* where he came from.

"Hey, Jack, how about you tell me what the hell you're talking about in American." Rupe was losing patience. Jack had about five minutes, because the first truck with his pumps was on the way.

"Okay," said Jack, "over 2,000 years ago, lead was used for all kinds of stuff in the ancient world. The Roman god Plumbus carried water in lead pipes. That's why we call it plumbing. That's why its symbol is Pb. The Greeks and Romans used white lead acetate for a sweetener in bitter wines to make them drinkable. They also used different kinds of molds and plants to help them talk to the gods. Back then they had a god for everything, kind of like our saints. It has been theorized that the man who wrote *The Iliad* and *The Odyssey* was using these substances in his diet when he wrote these stories. *The Iliad* was a famous, long Greek story that we studied in school. In my school, we studied it in Latin and had to learn to read *The Iliad* in that ancient language."

"Why?" said Rupe. "It's a language that nobody uses. Why would you want to waste time studying it?"

"I used it today," said Jack. "In these tales, the writer was as if he was walking in a dream state with the gods, and he would encounter fantastic sea monsters and giant fish that he would have to battle with, always out-smarting his enemy, meanwhile, always battling a monster within himself.

"Sometimes I feel like that if I eat day-old beans, the monster wants out…" Rupe smiled.

"I'm trying to explain this to you, knucklehead!" Jack was losing patience. "There are many things in nature, like opium, or marijuana, that have an effect on the human mind. Most of them are molds and fungi, but others are salts of metals, like that white powder that builds up on the mill and out on those tailings. That's akin to a drug in Goulard's Extract. It's a medicine used for cuts and infections, but if you eat it, you could get very sick. Do you remember ten or twelve years back --when all those workers died at that factory in New Jersey where they made the TEL?"

"Sure," said Rupe. "There was a big write-up in the *Mining Journal* about that. They said that the workers went mad, and that they saw angels and demons. Some were talking to the ceilings. The news said they died horrible deaths."

"That was from the lead compounds, the fumes from the boiling lead contain salts and they get into your brain and make you wacky."

"What does that have to do with plumbing?"

"The Romans used that lead white in bad wine that was usually consumed at orgies. It had an effect on the participants that, shall we say, cut the chains of propriety."

"American!" said Rupe. "Talk American, you crazy limey."

"It made them crazy so they would all fornicate!"

There was a few seconds delay as that sunk in.

"So you're saying they would eat this stuff?" Rupe was getting the picture.

"Mix it in the wine." Jack clarified.

"Okay, mix it in the wine, and then God would tell them to fuck each other?" Rupe was getting the point. "So what does that have to do with those guys in that Cadillac?" Rupe liked to keep things simple.

"Well," said Jack, "if I had to guess, I'd say, that German guy is going to slip somebody a mickey."

"Why didn't you just say that in the first place!" said Rupe. "All this bullcrap about that guy, Homer, and fighting monsters!" Rupe was piling it on now "You know, for an Englishman, you speak gibberish."

The roar of the big gasoline engines climbing the last grade into town could be heard as the men sat on the loading dock.

"Well, here come our pumps," said Rupe. "I've got my own monsters to battle with and they are down at the 700-foot level. Here come my reinforcements." He had his arms outstretched, pointing to the big GMC truck from Western Mine Supply, as it pulled up to the dock.

"Have you been eating the mountain jello?" Jack Asked.

"You know the rules, if it's not in my lunch pail, I don't eat it! Now if you'll excuse me, I have a mine to pump out." He smiled. "I don't have all day to entertain your wild notions about ancient Greece."

"Howdy…" Rupe waved hello to the truck driver coming out of the cab.

"Triumph Mine…" the driver said, handing a clipboard to Rupe.

"That's us, you bet," he said. And he signed the delivery receipt.

"Got some pretty big pumps here," said the driver, "they're heavy buggers."

Jack was barking orders at the men in the shop, "bring around the tow motor to off-load this equipment," as other men from inside the shop were gathering around to assist. Shiny, new equipment was always quick to draw attention. Once it was down in the hole, it would get covered with the same gray sludge as everything else, gray, with a white powdery trim.

Chapter Thirty-One

As the big, black Caddy eased onto Main Street in Ketchum, Averell saw a sister car exactly the same parked in front of the Alpine Bar.

"Let's pull in and have a drink," he told his driver.

The driver pulled a U-turn in the street and came up right behind the other Caddy.

"Come on," said Averell. "I want you to meet my friend, Posey."

The men piled out of the car and then through the swinging doors into the Alpine Bar.

A large mural was a work in progress behind the bar.

A young man from Philadelphia was sketching figures with charcoal on the canvas that stretched the whole back wall.

Averell quickly recognized Ernest, his press agent. The man next to him, George, was posing. The young artist, named Mike, drink in hand, was sketching George into the scene.

Ernest had already made his debut on the big mural and was pictured sitting on a chair, legs outstretched, on what appeared to be Main Street, Ketchum, in the late 1800's.

At the end of the bar, holding court as usual, was the grand patroness of the arts herself, Posey Gruner. She was wearing her silver cocktail dress, her hair was a platinum blond. She wore several, large diamonds and had a cigarette in a silver holder. She had a queenly prominence, in this, her joint, and every man was eager to please her.

Many were in her employ one way or another. There was George, her driver and handy man, and his assistant, Billy, also in the mural. Then there was John behind the bar, and a cook, several waitresses, none as pretty as Posey, she made sure of that.

Ernest was a regular, who, unlike most of her patrons, paid his tab, thanks to his contract with Averell.

Several other loggers and contract miners filled out the bar and the show was the mural. Everyone was a critic, as Mike sipped his Johnny Walker and worked the faces into his masterpiece.

Mike had arrived several months earlier and announced, after a half a bottle of scotch, that he was the best artist at *The Philadelphia Enquirer* and had been wrongly terminated for various improprieties, falsely and wrongly accused. Posey, recognizing an opportunity to support the arts and add some much needed culture to her joint, engaged his services for the greatest mural in the Northwest, or so it was said to be, if anyone was asking.

"Give him a jug," she barked orders at the young artist.

"I need some chow," said Mike. "I'm hungry."

"You're drunk," said Ernest. "You can't even hold your pencil."

Everyone laughed at the young man, but after hours, and early in the morning, he would return, coffee cup in hand, and tune up his scribbles into a western masterpiece that could rival anything back at the Philadelphia Art Museum. He was truly a master and he knew it.

Averell walked up to Posey and when she saw him she stood up and gave him a big hug and a kiss on his cheek. "Where have you been?" She said loud enough so everyone could hear. "You never come see me anymore."

"I stand before you now," he said. "I want you to meet some friends of mine. Gentlemen, I want you to meet The Queen of the Alpine, Posey Gruner. Posey this is Con Kelley of Anaconda Copper and this is the Baron von Tippelskirch from The Thyssen Steel Company, who is visiting us from Germany."

"Pleased to meet you both. John," she called to her bar manager, "set my guests up."

The three men settled in and watched the show as Mike drew faces on large pieces of drawing paper tacked to a board. The mural was primed at this point and was just three washes of color with figures and buildings penciled in. Three of the figures were further along, the two bearded miners at the bar were sketched in enough that is was clear who they were, and Ernest, Averell's press man, was seated to the left of what looked like the swinging doors of the Alpine, passed out.

"Mike," said Posey, "sketch Averell and his friends, be a doll. John, is Mike's lunch ready? The poor boy is starving. George, build up that fire, will you, and put something on jukebox. Let's liven this place up some."

Posey had money, and she had created a little kingdom for herself with many men under her control. All of them were hopeless drunks, but it was a life that was better than what she left behind. Her husband had died from what the doctors said was stomach cancer and Alzheimer's, but it was the exposure to chemicals in his lab that did it. He left her with a fortune in stocks and royalties from patents. She left Philadelphia society behind and had bought this place in hopes of forgetting her past.

Mike set up his board and had a new-styled Brownie box camera with a flash. He took several photos of all three men as Posey requested. He would then have them for reference and details later. He began to work a caricature of Averell's face.

"Don't mind him," Posey diverted Averell's attention. "So what have you boys been up to today?"

"We have been out to the Triumph. I wanted to show the baron the operation." Averell was nursing his bourbon.

"And how's that going? I hope you're making lots of money out there because I hear you're spending it on your ski area." Posey was pretty enough to slap Averell around and she knew it.

"Things are not that bad," he joked. "I think there are still a few gold bars in the storage cellar. Besides, we have the best press agent in New York." He toasted Ernest and the salute was graciously returned as Ernest was brought into what was light conversation.

"I love a good mug of German beer." Ernest was wading into it. "They make the best beer in the world, don't you think, Baron?"

"Ja-wohl." He wanted no trouble. "They do."

The two agreed.

"And they make the best steel too, the best hard steel in the world. They just don't make much in the way of petrol." Ernest had been drinking for awhile.

Posey took the conversation her way. "Are you a skier, Baron? Did Averell drag you up his mountain? I do hope you get that lift machine finished, Averell. I need customers and when it's finished, I will be the first stop for the lot of them after a hard day on that brute of a mountain."

The diversion was working. The guests were paying attention to her and not Ernest.

Mike was finishing up Averell's caricature and started on Mr. Kelley's, his hands dancing on the coarse paper like a magician. He had a tall stack of papers and sketches in his little work area at the other end of the bar.

"Yes, Madame, we skied yesterday and it was fantastic, very good." He was focusing his attention on her and away from Ernest's taunting.

"The baron raced all the way down with Zeppie. It was very exciting," said Averell.

"Racing?" said Posey. "How thrilling. I'm glad you didn't get hurt, Baron. I wouldn't want you going home with your legs in a cast." She was fishing and did not get a straight answer.

"No injuries, good skiing." He lifted his mug. "This is the best ski hill in the West." He toasted.

"Here, Here," said Mr. Kelley. It wasn't what Averell was looking for, he would settle for nothing less than the best in the world.

"I want you all to come to my 29th birthday party out at my private lodge in Baker Creek." She had been 29 for at least 10 years now. "We will have a Cat there. It will be the full moon. We expect to be able to night ski, weather-permitting. There will be the best catering company in the county there, and we have the nicest hot pool, not as big as yours, Averell, but you must admit, it's got a better view." She grabbed his hand and patted it. "Now, now, you can't always have the best."

"We will try to fit it in," he said.

Posey was insistent: "Your ski school will be there and many of the girls from the Hot Spring Hotel will be there. I'm going to have a cowboy band. It will be the event of the season. You simply must attend. I have a whole barrel of Walter Brostetter's red wine, and we are cooking lambs outside on big fires. I'm expecting a hundred people. I'll have buses leaving here at seven even, and they'll be coming back at one and two, so you don't even have to drive."

"Okay," said Averell, "we will be there, but I'm driving."

"I'm sorry," said Mr. Kelley, "but I have to return to Salt Lake tomorrow."

"Would you mind holding still for just a minute?" Mike pleaded. He had a few more details and he would have Mr. Kelley's face finished.

He would never get it onto the mural though. Mike began to expect deals for exposure to the mural. To get into the mural would be of some special value and men were vying for a spot in local history.

Averell and the men enjoyed the rustic break from the Lodge and the mine tour. It was a great adventure. The whole week had been and the baron was beginning to wish he could stay. He was in no rush to return to a continent hellbent on destruction. Nobody in their right mind wanted war, and he knew better than anyone where these raw materials were going.

Hitler had amassed a huge air force, like no other the world had ever seen. The purchase of 500 tons of lead and twenty million dollars in aircraft fuel, which was the purpose of his business trip, would allow the Nazi air war to proceed.

This purchase was critical to the Fatherland. The baron had made the deal, the material was being processed, the supply line was verified and he could afford to relax some.

Chapter Thirty-Two

Averell returned to his room for the evening, as did the others. At ten o'clock the phone in Averell's room rang. It was the hotel switchboard operator.

"Mr. Harriman, you have an overseas long distance call."

"Put it through, operator."

The line was crackling and the caller was hard to understand. "Mr. Harriman," a thick, German accent sounded far away. "This is Fritz Thyssen. I must talk quickly. This line may go dead. Things have changed here and I'm having my doubts about some decisions I have made."

"What kinds of doubts, Fritz. Business seems very good. We have made accommodations in our raw material deliveries to fill this fuel order." Averell was detecting a genuine fear.

The phone was scratchy, but they could understand each other. Germany was halfway around the world from Idaho, over 6,000 miles, and the fact that they were talking at all was a marvel of modern technology.

"I'm beginning to think that I backed a mad man," said Fritz. "At first I was sure he would be a good thing for my country and German industry. The two parties were deadlocked on all decisions, the workers' unions were pushing us towards communism, I thought this man Hitler could unify us, and he did, but now I have serious doubts and I believe my life is in danger."

"How could that be?" said Averell. "You're the head of the largest industrial machine in the world, Fritz." Averell had always done business with Fritz Thyssen and was taken off guard by this information.

"Mr. Harriman, things have gone too far here. We need to consider severing our business dealings somehow. This must come from your side of the Atlantic. I no longer have control of my operations here," he said.

"Well, who does, sir?" Averell was astonished by this remark.

"We have become a military state, Mr. Harriman. I now am quite sure that we are headed down a very dark path. I am considering leaving. I must go now. I implore you, find a way to cut off trade with our factories here. It's very likely that we will not be able to pay our bills. Good night and God help us."

The phone went dead, there was just static. Averell hung up his receiver and lay on his bed, looking up at the ceiling.

The two men both held up in their own private castles. Averell in his concrete hotel, high in the Idaho mountains, and Fritz, in his 15th century castle, high in the German Alps-- industrialists, focusing on trade, on producing high quality products, maintaining hundreds of thousands of jobs. We produce steel he thought. We can't be responsible for how it is used. We can't be responsible for evil in the world. He thought about his week, the skiing was very good, the movie was progressing, and his resort was going to be a success.

Germany was a world away. Hitler couldn't threaten him here, or in New York, for that matter. But in fact, German submarines were already cruising the East Coast and collecting information.

Hitler knew he would have trouble ruling the world without dealing with America and Averell knew that Germany could not fly without lead. The world could be an ugly place, but not here, not in his mountain retreat, here everything was white, and pure, and clean and he was going to keep it that way.

Chapter Thirty-Three

Mikel, the artist also known locally as just "Mike", had most of his characters penciled in: Averell and Bunny earned spots. Ernest, Bill, John, George, some of the miners and Angel, the head waitress, along with her friend Becky, had managed to earn a place in barroom history, as well.

Mikel had been making all kinds of side deals with everyone he could: the bartenders, the waitresses. Billy had granted him use of his horse for his position, and then there was his deal with Ernest for an old shotgun.

On a recent bird-hunting excursion in the lowlands, the gun refused to fire and the two men got into an argument and Ernest demanded that he be removed from the masterpiece.

"I can't help it if you can't shoot." Ernest said. "I don't give a god damn if I'm in your painting or not."

And with that, Mike put in the pony that Billy had given him the use of, dead center--a little, swayback pinto, trailing dutifully behind Billy, leaving nothing but Ernest's long legs and his big boots sticking out under the horse's head.

Mikel slapped the gun back down on the bar, "Take it," he said in a feisty burst. "The damn thing doesn't work."

Little would he know, twenty years later, Ernest would take that old gun into his den for a cleaning, and unfortunately, it would work.

149

The colors were going on now and everyone at the bar was amazed. Even the loudest critics would sit quietly, sipping their beers, watching the paint fill the voids on the long canvas.

Posey was very pleased. Her joint was graced with a little class. "Mike," she said, "you are the best, and *The Saturday Evening Post* has got nothing on you. I bet Averell could make a phone call and get you on one of the New York papers."

She knew the project would end soon and he would become a hopeless drunk in her entourage of alcoholics and hangers on. She wanted better for him and she vowed to approach Averell on the issue at the party, if he came.

Chapter Thirty-Four

Friday, December 17, 1938. At six o'clock, two buses sat in front of the Alpine with their engines running and the heaters on.

George was already up at Baker Creek. The little Cat had labored all day to open the road good enough for the bus to drive into the field just below the cabin. George had plowed a parking lot big enough for 50 or 60 cars and room to turn around. Then he plowed a large, open spot in the back of the cabin for a bon fire and cooking fires.

After that was done, he set up a large steel tripod with a chain and hook. On this, the caterers set a heavy, black kettle, about 30 gallons. There were two cooking spits to either side of the cook kettle that would hold a small steer and a lamb.

Posey also had about a ton of hay delivered and after spreading some on the ground, Bill and George put the rest, in a big circle, around the bonfire and cooking fires.

The little glen was bordered by large pines and the cabin had been decorated for the holidays. They brought prepared ingredients from the bar's kitchen in several large tins. There were three-foot and four-foot pine fire logs delivered and stacked for the bonfire, and a cord of dry Aspen wood for the cooking fires, split and stacked.

At five o'clock, the cook fires were started and the pine wood was piled into a teepee-shaped cone ready to light when the guests arrived.

The main room of the cabin was set with a long table with a very large, silver punch bowl and cups that would hold hot, spiced wine.

At sunset, George ran the Cat up the hill behind the cabin that had several good wide ski trails left by loggers. Posey had paid them to make them suitable for skiing and then had George remove the stumps with the Cat during the summer.

At the top of the mountain, she had the loggers build her a three-sided structure, with a stone fireplace, to get in out of the wind.

In some ways she was lonely and alone since her husband had passed so she surrounded herself with the best friends that money could buy. Tonight there would be a hundred of them.

At about eight o'clock, the Idaho sky began to light up. In an hour, the full moon would dominate the winter sky and reflect off the snow so brightly that it was almost like day.

The Cat sat resting, its fuel tank was topped off and a thick 200-foot rope was tied to the back of the machine. They expected at least thirty people would want to ski.

Some would not go to the top, but would still bring their skis and trek on over to the hot springs, a mile away.

At six o'clock, the fires were set, the caterers arrived and began preparing the food and wine.

At seven o'clock, the guests began to arrive. A well-spaced line of cars could be seen down the valley. Two of the cars were V16 Caddy's and one was a little Bantam pickup.

The bus was full of folks from town who had no intention of driving home. Their skis were in the racks on the side of the bus.

As the cars began to pull into the parking lot, George began to think he should have made it bigger.

"Owooooow..." The girls coming off the bus let out a yelp that echoed in the big valley. It was a cool night, but not cold, the air was still, the temperature was in the mid-20's, couldn't be better for a winter party. They all could smell the pine burning as they were drawn up the yard toward the fires like moths.

Most of the guests wore ski boots. They were warm and well-suited for standing on the cold ground, whether they chose to ski or not.

The party was becoming an annual event and each year more people would come. This was the third year they'd done it and it made Posey feel very special and gave her a sense of family, even though many of her extended family were just employees. She was good to them, and this yearly event was a thank you.

The food was laid out like a royal banquet. The cooking fires were attended by John and Bill from the Alpine. The bar back in town was closed for the night, a simple sign hung on the door: *Closed for the Baker Creek Party.*

The band set up under the back porch, next to a small coal-oil heater. There was a fiddle, a stand-up bass and a guitar. They started playing cowboy songs, and the little glen came alive.

The baron had never seen anything like this before. A party of this size would have been formal in his homeland. This was more on the level of a peasant farm-village, harvest feast, except they were going to ski. That was different.

It was almost an hour before that moon would take the sky. In the meantime, folks loosened up. Many of the guests brought flasks, some just had a bottle in a brown paper bag. The main table in the lodge held a very large and ornate silver punch bowl, set on a Sterno heater. It was filled with hot wine with slices of oranges in it.

There was cheese, cakes, bread, lots of finger foods prepared by the cook that Posey had hired for the occasion.

"Hot wine," said Rowdey, as he and Annie walked to the table.

"Okay, I'll try some," she said. "This is quite the deal."

"Yea, she does it every year, and it keeps getting bigger." He handed her a cup of hot wine.

The little band kicked into *Ragtime Cowboy Joe* and some of the ladies began to dance with one willing young man.

"I'll give you a dollar for that hat, cowboy," an Austrian accent boomed from across the plowed yard. It was Audie and he was in his best ski clothes, ready for a big night. He looked like a character right out of the Tyrol: Heavy wool ski pants, a heavy wool sweater from the old country, and very expensive black leather ski boots. His big smile was infectious,

"Not for sale," Rowdey responded. "But I might let you wear it awhile if you promise not to yodel."

The two men were both in the best of moods and greeted each other like old friends, even though they had only bumped into each other occasionally at the Alpine. Rowdey knew these guys were good skiers and he respected them for that. It was their way of life, in some ways, he was a little envious.

The crowd loosened up and continued to grow. A big Lincoln limo rolled into the lot and struggled to find room to park. Several over-dressed Californians piled out and made their way to the fire--one older man and three very pretty actresses in long, heavy fur coats, the man in raccoon and the ladies in mink.

They were definitely over-dressed, but once they found a place near the big fire, they fit right in.

The man lit up a series of hand-rolled cigarettes and began to pass them around the circle of the big fire. The smell of reefer mixed with pine and floated up towards the rising moon.

The band played *Don't Fence Me In* and some of the revelers sang along. The song caught the spirit of the American West, lots of space, no rules except the cowboy way, a simple code of ethics, mixed with a deep respect for Mother Nature.

Across the Atlantic, the world was ready to unleash the dogs of hell. Here, the coyotes sang along with the band.

"Well, Baron," said Bunny, "are you having fun on our little trip?"

"Ya," said the baron. "I don't want to leave, but I must."

"Tomorrow, at noon," said Bunny. "We have a window in the weather and a wind at our tail."

"I will be back in Germany in a few days. I'm not looking forward to it." The baron was suddenly confessing to his associate. "We are marching to war," he said. "War is hell. It always has been and always will be. Win or lose, it's hell. I would rather stay here."

The joint was passed to him and he passed it on without comment or concern. He took out his silver flask, "Schnapps?" He looked at Bunny.

"Oh, thanks, I'm a Kentucky Bourbon man." Bunny took a pull on his brown, leather flask.

The two men had traveled the world and seen opium and hashish commonly smoked in the Middle East and the Orient. "Everybody has their poison, eh, Baron?" Bunny smiled a big understanding smile.

"Ja-wohl," said the baron, while the band played *Pretty Redwing* and more people began to dance.

The fires blazed on and the moon showed its first edge over the mountains behind them as the Boulders lit up in reds and dark purples. They were so steep that snow couldn't even hang on their bare rock faces.

Chapter Thirty-Five

The moon was halfway up when George fired up the little Cat. "Anyone planning on skiing should get ready," he called out over the ever-loudening crowd.

"Are you coming, cowboy?" said Audie. "Tonight, you get to ride with the big boys."

"Last I looked…" Rowdey said, "I'm taller than you. I guess I'll have to come along and make sure you don't hurt yourself."

The group of about twenty people began to gather around the tow line of the Cat. Averell and Bunny were first in line. This was going to be a new experience for them and they wouldn't miss it.

"I need to find the water closet," said the baron to his hosts. "I'll be right back."

As the baron entered the main room with the food table and the wine, he removed the hotel envelope that he had folded in his coat pocket. It contained the white powdered lead salts and the dried remains of the mold that he removed from the Triumph on the tour. He was careful not to attract attention to himself as he took the large silver ladle and put the contents from the envelope in it. Then he dipped the ladle in the hot wine and watched the powder dissolve.

As a student of chemistry at the University of Munster, his college buddies often experimented with psychotropic compounds. There was a great interest in ritual sexual rites in ancient Egypt and it was discovered that molds and salts were often used for what could only be described as a wild night on the town. These compounds have been used throughout the ages by priests and wizards, and as Homer wrote, "they tend to loosen your tongue and untie your inhibitions."

The baron saw the opportunity to collect the compounds hoping for an opportunity to use them, but he never thought one so well-suited as this would present itself. No one would get hurt or sick, they would just feel a little more randy than usual and elements in the surroundings would be more vivid.

Things were already pretty vivid and it wasn't going to take much to get this crowd randy. They were already off to a good start with bourbon and reefer.

"Would you like some wine?" the baron was fixed on the attractive woman in the full-length mink.

"Oh, thank you," she said. "It's hot."

"Yes, it is," said the baron, "just like you must be in that beautiful coat. I have to go, enjoy the wine.

People had worked up an appetite and were fixing plates. The baron hurried outside to join the skiing group. He was locking on his skis when George gave a bump to the idler on the Caterpillar.

"All aboard," said George.

And the skiers found a place on the big rope. Rowdey and Annie stayed near the very end, with Audie and two of his Austrian buddies. Averell, Bunny, and the baron were near the front. There were about fifteen men and five women.

"Hold on," said George. "Here we go…"

The little machine crawled forward in low gear until everyone was settled in. They were spaced about 15 feet apart and had no problem holding on. The trail was not as steep as

Bald Mountain. It was a nice, gentle hill with a big wide trail, almost a 150 feet across, cut through a thick pine forest. There was plenty of snow, the Cat track was cut and the crowd on the line just had to hang on.

Up the hill they went, into a heavy, pine forest. The lighting was very good and you could see as well or better than on any cloudy day.

George had to stop on some of the tighter turns and let people realign to the track, but all and all, it went pretty smoothly.

The group of nocturnal adventurers headed up the hill and finally arrived at the little shed at the top. The air was still and the view was breathtaking, 360 degrees around, nothing but snow-covered peaks and heavily-timbered hillsides.

The moon had taken the sky and had a mild, red glow that cast a faint pink reflection on the snow. That would fade as it climbed higher.

The gang began to pack down the fresh snow around the mountain shed as George lit the fire and used a small can of diesel fuel to bring it to a roar. The skiers huddled around. The area was packed and they removed their skis and leaned them up against the shed or stuck them into the deep snow.

Averell, Bunny, and the baron stood outside. They continued to share flasks of Schnapps and bourbon, but they were by no means feeling it. They were just warmed by the brew and loving the adventure.

"Someday we will have chairlifts all over this ground." Bunny told the baron.

"In my homeland we have cog trains to take you up the mountains," he bragged, "they work very well and they are heated."

"Heated," said Averell. "What's next, a dining car?"

They laughed.

"It's possible," said the baron. "We love skiing in the Alps, he continued, "it's our national pastime."

"It's as close as we can get to flying," said Averell.

The group in the shed was warming up and the fire was lighting up the whole area with a yellow glow. Audie and Rowdey were huddled up with Annie and staring at big logs.

"I wish I could stay here forever," said Annie. "The air is so clean here, life is so clean here," she said.

"It doesn't have to be," said Audie, "the land I left is just as beautiful as this and people are turning on each other, over money, religion, power, god knows what else. The world can turn on itself. I'm afraid for those in my homeland, especially the Jews..."

"Why the Jews?" said Rowdey. "What did they do?"

"They were too successful. They worked harder. They stayed together in a group and they were moneylenders. So when the economy slowed down and farmers and workers couldn't pay the money they borrowed, it was easy to make them a target." Audie was suddenly back in Austria, thinking of his home town of Vienna, a prosperous city that had fallen prey to the same depression that was griping the US.

The banks were all connected, and the world-wide depression would bring out the worst in man: War.

World War II had begun on the other side of the globe and it drove hundreds of thousands of people out of Central Europe; over 300,000 Jews were in Austria alone. Half were lucky to get out with the clothes on their back. Many went to Britain, but most made their way to America.

Even those Austrians with one Jewish grandparent would be considered a Jew and forced into work camps. Did any of the Austrians that were in Sun Valley fall into that bracket? Hell, half of Europe could fall into that bracket, if you searched family trees. It was like a wild fire, or a cancer, where man as a species was self-destructing.

"You know," Audie wanted to change the subject because it was pulling him down, "I love to ski. Don't you?" He looked into Annie's eyes and for the first time both her and Rowdey saw him as something other than a foreigner.

"Yes. Yes, I do," said Annie, in a matter of fact kind of way."

"I love to ski," he paused.

"To skiing…" said Rowdey, and he lifted his small bottle of peach port, wrapped in a brown paper bag. They passed it around and it warmed them as the fire blasted on.

They could see the fires down below and hear the band playing and the people dancing. They could also see the smoke from the hot springs off in the distance, and in between there, was a group of several people in what looked like long coats walking back down the trail towards the hot springs.

"Well, are we going to ski, or we gonna stand by the fire all night?" said Rowdey.

Averell heard that remark from outside the lean-to.

"Let's ski," he said.

"Ya," said the baron. And the group slowly began to move from the fire back to their equipment.

161

Chapter Thirty-Six

Annie was the first out of the shed, and she pushed off into the light dusting of fresh snow. The baron was next, then Audie close behind him.

The baron and Audie had not said a word to each other, but they both knew they were from the Fatherland. Audie had heard about the race from Zep and, of course, in that version, Zep had won by a nose.

It was close now, but they were in no mood for a challenge. They had been drinking. It was night. They came around the first long gentle turn and could see about a mile of steady, wide trail in front of them that led to the hot pool.

Everyone held up on the ridge, looking out at the Boulders. Then Annie said, "Last one to the hot pool is a rotten egg."

"What is this rotten egg?" said the baron.

"Not me," said Bunny. "I've got to be at my office in two days."

"I have to be home in three," said the baron.

Annie took off, followed by Rowdey and a few others in the crowd. The rest watched, perched on the top of the grade, as the skiers' tails left wisps of white dust. The snow was soft and nobody got going very fast.

"Shall we..." said Bunny.

"Hot pool or cabin?" said Averell.

"Cabin for me," said Bunny.

The three men, along with some of the others in the party, headed back to the cabin. The band was playing and the smoke was hanging over the snow-covered glen, refusing to rise.

As they skied up to the back porch of the little lodge, they could see most of the crowd from the backyard was gone.

"Where is everybody?" wondered Bunny.

"I don't know," said Averell. "But I'm hungry."

They had been gone about an hour or so and in that time the revelers, mostly women, had consumed the bulk of the big, silver, hot wine bowl. There was nothing but some orange rinds left and what looked like a teaspoon of sand in the bottom of the silver vessel.

Bunny was somewhat surprised when he entered the big room of the cabin. The fire was dying down, the lights were low and the people inside were all wrapped up like a big ball of snakes, during mating season.

"What the hell…" said Averell.

"That must have been opium they were smoking," said Bunny. He had traveled the Far East and seen opium dens and geisha halls. Many of the women were undressed and all over each other, men too, but most of the men had gone skiing so the room was mostly full of women, and they were obviously drugged.

Some just lay back on the floors, coats were scattered like rugs, others were off in the bedrooms, and the men that were there were engaged in sex with two or more women, who were talking nonsense. The whole affair was like a Roman orgy.

The band was not sure what to do, so they played on, but they slowed it down. They were playing a slow version of the Eddy Duchin hit *Let's Fall In Love,* but from where they were standing, it didn't look like love was happening. Nobody would believe this in the morning.

The baron was both surprised and disappointed. He didn't expect the small amounts of powder he collected would have such an effect and he was sorry all the wine was gone. It must have been the mold, he thought, even though it dried out, it still had the alkaloids.

Averell went looking for something to eat. John was still out by the cook fires. He was sitting on an unsplit piece of cordwood in front of a large pot of strong coffee.

"Any food left?" said Averell. "What the hell happened in there?"

"Try some of the lamb," said Posey. She was wrapped in a heavy wool, Indian blanket and a long, red-striped wool coat, seated on a straw bail in front of the big fire pit. Carla sat on a bail next to her and they had finished a bottle of champagne. The two had been talking about the big city and had bonded some.

"What happened in there?" Averell asked

"I think somebody pulled a Mickey Finn on my party," she said.

"Yea, a big Mickey," said Carla. "I like sex as much as the next girl…"

"Yeah?" said Posey. The champagne made them both giddy. "I'm just old-fashioned. I don't think it's a team sport."

"Yea," said Carla, "I guess we're a couple of nuns."

They laughed and huddled closer. The two women had both been around and just thought the whole thing was kinky and funny.

"My party's going to be the talk of the town now," she said.

"I wouldn't be surprised if it gets into Time Magazine."

"That will never happen. I'll make sure of that." Averell was sure of that.

"Here ya go," said John, he handed Averell a plate of lamb with some baked beans and a metal cup of strong black coffee.

"Thanks," said Averell.

Bunny went looking for Margie. He found her in a back bedroom, face down in a pile of coats. One of the old miners was huddled up behind her. They were both naked as jaybirds.

At first he was going to make a scene, but then he thought better of it. He suddenly felt responsible. He should never have left her alone. As they were both passed out cold, he just closed the door and went back to the fire.

Chapter Thirty-Seven

Over at the hot springs, Audie sat in the hot pool between the Hollywood girls. Their expensive fur coats lay on the snow, like big brown animals curled up.

Rowdey and Annie were across the pool, side by side. Although they were all naked, they were respectful of each other.

The man with the big Lincoln was in the pool, his arms outstretched on the warm rocks. He was just looking up at the moon. The opium put him in a state of bliss.

"Anyone want some peach port?" said Rowdey.

"Sure…" said the platinum blond.

They passed it around the pool.

"What a night," said Rowdey.

"Ya," Audie had to agree. He was naked in a hot pool on the side of a mountain wilderness with two hot blonds that were well into the tank and feeling no pain, a passed-out guy, and two, new friends. His decision to come to Sun Valley was a good path. He was a lover, not a fighter, and had he stayed in Austria, he would have resisted and ended up dead in a ditch like so many thousands of his countrymen.

"Well," said Rowdey, "It is date night. I think Annie and I are going to retire. I'll leave you here and I'm sure you'll be fine."

When Annie rose up from the pool to dress, Audie was aroused and the platinum blond somehow sensed it. Maybe it was the tightening of his muscles. She slipped her hand between his legs and the other girl began to whisper in his ear. As Annie and Rowdey put their skis back on to trek back to the cabin, the second woman mounted Audie.

"Do you think he'll be okay?" said Annie.

"I hope so." Rowdey chuckled. "Maybe I should jump in and save him."

Annie smacked him, "Giddy up, cowboy." And the two left Audie behind.

The two women were all over him as the other man continued to stare up at the moon in an opiated-stupor.

When Annie and Rowdey got back to the cabin, they headed for the fire. Averell had built it back up and the gang sat around it, drinking coffee and eating some of the lamb.

The guests had not eaten much because they got into the hot wine and before they knew what hit them, they were all dirty dancing.

"What happened, where is everybody?" said Annie.

The band finally gave up and was packing up.

Ernest came out on the back porch, pulling up his suspenders, "I could eat a horse," he announced. The crowd inside was beginning to rustle.

"Well, if it ain't the big bull elk of the woods," said Posey, "did you give your herd a good working over, studly." She got right in his face.

"I think someone spiked the punch," said Ernest.

"Ya think?!!!" They all chimed in unison.

"That was a first for me," he laughed. "I think I'm going to church this morning."

"Yeah, the church bells are calling your name." Posey laughed.

Chapter Thirty-Eight

On a small knoll above the cabin, a sniper lay on a white blanket, holding his Mosin–Nagant m1891/30 with a powerful scope. The rifle was Russian, but it was made in America by Remington. The man who called himself Arthur was really Morris Cohen, a Russian national born in the port town of Murmansk. He was a US citizen and member of the Communist Party in New York City.

The Russian intelligence network had been following TEL production very closely and was well aware of the US industrial connections with Ford and GM. Russia had a peace treaty with Germany, but Stalin certainly didn't expect Hitler to honor it. The fuel was the key to Germany's airpower and had to be stopped.

Morris was born into a merchant family that dealt with fuel and lubricants throughout the Northern European continent. His father traded with the Turkish Shell Oil offices and dealt mostly with heavy oils used for ships and trains. Comrade Cohen had learned of the patent conflicts over TEL and dealt with trade in thinner solvents.

Morris was supposed to have taken out the baron in New York, but he just couldn't get a clean opportunity. He followed the baron, then he followed Carla, and managed to get a flight plan from a mechanic at Teterboro in New Jersey.

This could be his last chance tonight to take out the baron. He could not just follow them back tomorrow. He had to travel to Twin Falls and pick up a flight to Kansas, then New York. He had no way of moving as fast as they. It was now or never.

He set the rifle on the blanket and wiped it down. He was wearing a pair of thin white gloves under his heavy mittens. The plan was to take the shot, leave the rifle in the snow and ski off to his car at the highway. The gun was disposable and he did not want to get caught, but if he was caught, he would be handed over to the Russian Consulate anyway. What mattered is that he completed his mission.

Chapter Thirty-Nine

Averell, Posey, and Carla sat at the fire pit. Averell was finishing his plate.

"Good cooking, John," he said, "this lamb is delicious. What's the secret?"

"Sagebrush," said John. "I toss sagebrush on the cooking fire, old Indian trick." John was smiling. "Coffee?"

"We could all use some," said Averell. He was looking at Carla and Posey. "Well ladies, did we have fun tonight?"

"I'll say," said Posey. "This is one for the record books." She was staring at the fire.

The baron didn't expect so sudden a reaction to his chicanery, had he known, he would have waited. By the time they returned from skiing, the crowd had all reacted to the chemicals in their own way: some had become very talkative, except the words coming out of their mouths were not comprehensible, like talking in tongues; others began to preach, some sang, some flapped around on the floor like fish out of water.

After that initial burst of emotion, they all needed to be held, so they all began to grope and roll around like the citizens in a Roman orgy.

As the animal within them became aroused, they began to couple anyway they could. At times, it almost looked like a conga dance. They looked like a room possessed.

The band was freaked out. They were drinking beer so they just played on. The girls from the Lodge all drank the hot wine, and so did the bus driver. He was a married man with kids, just picking up some overtime. Many of the people at the party would not want what happened to get around.

As they began to awake and find their clothes in the piles on the floor, some made their way out to the bonfire, seeking coffee. Most were in a state of shock.

It was about midnight; the moon was high in the sky past its peak.

Chapter Forty

The shooter was as still as a setter on point. He had a shell in the chamber. He had a small thermos of hot coffee in his rucksack and the white, winter suit he was wearing was very warm. He could easily sit there all night.

He understood the importance of his mission, but was not sure killing the baron would make any difference regarding the supply delivery. The ship would have to be seized or destroyed and that was the job of other resistance members.

The oil industry had so many arrangements and supply contractors worldwide, it was difficult to follow them.

Germany was trading with Africa and the Turkish, through Royal Dutch Shell and through Russia and North Sea companies. Stalin and Hitler had a peace treaty, neither one trusted each other, but that didn't stop them from doing business.

Heavy crude was used for heating oil and diesel trucks and generators, but the TEL was what made warplanes fly and Stalin didn't want Hitler's air force in his air space.

Stalin had close to five-thousand I-15 and I-16 fighters that had broken numerous flight speed records, but when the German aircraft industry had delivered the *Messerschmitt bF-109* to the Spanish Civil War, it dealt a decisive blow to the Russian Air Squadrons.

Hitler had produced over twenty-thousand of these new planes, but didn't have fuel to fly them. Stalin's only chance was to keep Germany from getting fuel.

Little did Comrade Cohen know that many of the contacts he was working with were being purged by Stalin as he sat in the snow up Baker Creek. He was working for an ungrateful master, who would keep a network of idealists working in the US, out of New York mostly. But Stalin got rid of any free thinkers in his inner circle.

The amount of tonnage that would be used for the World War II military buildup was staggering. The US out-built the world in aircraft. The German Air Command had 109,000 planes, Russia had 125,000.

Within a few years, the United States would build 325,000 aircraft of superior quality, mostly by women, and they all flew on high-octane fuel using TEL.

A world of pawns, thrown into the fray for a few kings gone mad.

Chapter Forty-One

As the baron moved back to the bonfire, he moved along side of Rowdey.

"You are a very good skier," he said.

"Thanks, buddy," said Rowdey. "I ski down from the mine several nights a week so I get a fair amount of practice."

"I would like to ask a small favor," said the baron.

"What's that?" Rowdey was suddenly wary. "I would like to buy your hat. I would like to take it home with me." He said.

"No way, pal, but you could buy a brand new one in town. I've had this one a long time and it's broken in to fit my lumpy head," he smiled, "here ya go, try it on."

The two men switched hats, Rowdey wearing a heavy German wool hat and the baron finally sporting a cowboy hat.

"Schnapps?" he said.

"Oh, what the hell," said Rowdey, "why not?"

The two men were both wearing dark, winter wool coats and from where the sniper sat, 300 yards away, he was suddenly confused.

It was getting late and there were clouds moving in, maybe a storm. He couldn't be sure, but it was warm enough to snow. If he lost the moonlight, he might miss his opportunity. He steadied his rifle, took a deep breath and pulled the trigger.

The rifle cracked the mountain night and Rowdey felt a spear shoot through his upper left chest, dropping him into the fire. The men pulled him out instantly and laid him down on the straw-covered snow.

"Where did that shot come from?" said John, a skilled hunter.

The group scattered, headed for cover. Averell took the girls inside. George ran to the Caddy and pulled his rifle out of the trunk. John ran for his gun and a first aid kit that he kept in his truck.

Annie was applying pressure on Rowdey's wound and had quickly removed her coat, sweater and shirt. Then she tore her shirt to get rags for a bandage.

In the heat and chaos of it all, Comrade Morris Cohen, an accomplished athlete, took off through the woods on his skies and made it quickly back to his car.

He tossed the skies over the snowbank, started his car and pulled on down the highway, waiting a mile before he turned his lights on.

Rowdey lay on a heavy blanket near the fire. John had banked it again to a steady blaze.

"Get me some whiskey," said Annie.

"Should I call the sheriff?" said George.

"Hell, no!" said Posey. "There's been enough trouble here already tonight. We don't need to have this spread all over the paper... Besides, there's no phone up here. We've got to get him into town."

"He's going to be okay," said Annie. "The bullet went clean through his bicep muscle and out the outer side. His bone is not broken, though it might be chipped. We will need to get him to a doctor." Her pre-med at Princeton was finally paying off.

"That shot was for me," said the baron.

"It sure was," said Averell. "We need to get you out of here and fast. Posey, do you think you can handle this?" He looked into his old friend's eyes.

"This isn't my first rodeo, Averell. Our cowboy had a little hunting accident while cleaning his gun. Me and the sheriff go back some, you go on."

She understood how an incident like this could look for a man like Averell Harriman. The press would have a field day, especially if they interviewed anybody that had some of that wine.

Averell gathered his entourage. Carla said goodbye to her new friend and Posey gave her a hug. Annie had cleaned the wound and bandaged it, the blood was already congealing, and Rowdey looked like he was stabilized.

"I guess I won't be mining tomorrow," Rowdey was always the joker. Still want to buy that hat?" He was looking a little shaken.

"I'm sorry, cowboy," said the baron. "Yes, I would. It might become my lucky hat," and he handed Rowdey the rest of his American travel money in a silver clip with a strange symbol stamped into the silver. There was a stack of several hundred dollars there, easy. "Good luck to you," he said.

"Let's go," said Averell.

And they headed back to town.

"What a god damn night." Rowdey sat up and got to a hay bail. "This is gonna hurt like hell in the morning."

"It is morning," said Annie. "We need to get you to a hospital. I'm pretty sure your okay. It's so cold that I doubt there will be much chance of infection, but you still need to get a tetanus shot and that will need to be examined and stitched, you need that arm." She was trying to lighten the tone of things.

"Yea, it comes in handy." He gave her a squeeze with his good arm but he had no strength. John and some members of the band got the injured young man into the back of Posey's limo but buy the time the big black car was warmed up and turned around, Rowdey was dead.

Annie was in a state of shock. How could things go so wrong? That shot was meant for the German, not her man.

About halfway back to town, the full brunt of the event hit her and she broke into uncontrollable tears. Posey's big black limo had turned into a hearse. She and Posey now had a funeral to plan.

Chapter Forty-Two

When Averell got back to the hotel, his team kicked into service mode.

Bunny called the hanger at Gimlet. "Lyle, this is Bunny Bush. We flew in on the BC3. I need you to get that aircraft ready to go right away, and Lyle, give it an extra check over, look for any kind of tampering, just in case." Bunny didn't want to make a scene.

"I can have her ready for first light or sooner, sir," said Lyle, ready to accommodate his best customers.

"Start it and let it warm up. We will be there in an hour," Bunny said.

Averell called to Carla's room. "Toss your things into a bag as quickly as you can. We will stop in Salt Lake and you can freshen up there. Find Ernest and have him handle the local paper, there will be an incident report, so have him quash it, hunting accident or misfire, I don't care. The boy is a casualty of war and there is no bullet. Tell him to handle it, that's what we pay him for. I don't want any PR problems with this."

"Yes, sir, Mr. Harriman."

Averell was suddenly feeling a bit negligent. Hindsight is always 20/20, but he should have considered that someone might be tracking one of Germany's top generals. New York was crawling with spies: Russian Spies, Spanish Freedom Fighters, German Spies, British Agents, Jap and chinnie spies. The city was a world trade center with a consulate for every major and minor country on the planet.

Commodities were traded in huge quantities everyday and it was Brown Brothers Harriman's job to make money for the shareholders, no matter who they were. If the board began to judge deals on moral merit, they would never get anything done, and a competitor would just roll over them.

They traded commodities: steel, aluminum, lead, zinc, timber, chemicals—every day, no questions asked.

Chapter Forty-Three

At about 4:30 a.m., the Lodge limo pulled out onto the tarmac of the private airport at Gimlet. Lyle was in the cockpit, the plane was running, wheel chocks in place. Lyle was checking the instruments. All the lights were on, including the runway lights and the hanger lights.

The moon was still lingering, lighting the surrounding mountains. The sky was clear.

"Looks like we've got a good flying day," said Averell.

"Saddle up." The baron was still wearing his new, very used, hat.

Carla tossed her travel bag to Bunny, who was setting things in the baggage locker at the rear of the plane. The Lodge driver was loading the heavy luggage bags in the belly compartment of the plane.

Averell and Lyle switched seats.

"She's good to go, sir," said Lyle. "She checked out fine. Fueled. All your gauges check. You're cleared to Salt Lake and onto New York via Kansas City. Have a safe trip, sir, and we'll see ya soon."

"Thanks, Lyle." Averell shook his hand and placed a twenty dollar bill in his palm. The two men exchanged a wink and a nod.

Lyle climbed down the flight ladder and closed the door. Bunny latched it from inside and Lyle tapped on the door from the outside, pulled the wheel chocks and gave a thumbs-up to Averell in the cockpit.

The twin engines idled up as the plane began to roll out to the single runway. Averell pushed the double throttle forward and the silver aircraft took off and up into the pre-dawn sky.

As it climbed out of the Wood River Valley and up over the lava fields of the great Idaho Batholith, they saw an almost empty highway below, but for one lone car headed south towards Twin Falls.

Chapter Forty-Four

The sheriff walked into the Alpine at about eleven on the following day. Posey was not looking forward to the meeting, but as always, she was cordial and had John bring Sheriff Howes a cup of coffee, black.

"Hello, Posey," said the sheriff. "I heard things got a little wild and woolly up at Baker Creek last night." He was easing on into his investigation.

"Yes they did, Sheriff, but I had nothing to do with the shooting. I hate guns and don't carry one. John does."

The Sheriff had known John since childhood and the two men were old friends. "What happened, John?" The sheriff was expecting an answer that would complete his report.

"I'm not really sure what happened, Sheriff." John was being honest, kind of. "There was a shot from somewhere. No shooter and we can't find a gun. The kid works at the Triumph, is a good kid. I wish I could give you more information, but that is all I know.

"Who was there, John," The sheriff could sense that he wasn't getting the whole story.

"Me, George, Posey, a busload of locals and Sun Valley Company maids and waiters, a couple of California Hollywood types, some of the ski instructors and Ernest.

Ernest was at the end of the bar nursing a headache with a cup of hot coffee.

"Must've had a big time last night, Ernest." The sheriff got a little deeper into it. "Not too often I see you with coffee so close to lunch."

Ernest didn't bite. "I think I'm getting the flu." he said.

"Were you in the hot pool last night?" the sheriff asked.

"No. I stayed out of it, but there were a lot of people there and maybe I caught something from one of them." Ernest lied.

"Maybe you did," the Sheriff scratched his balls and gave John a wink.

John laughed some, but it was a poor attempt, and it only made the Sheriff more certain that he was not getting a full story. Fact was he didn't give a shit what went on out there as long as nobody got hurt. He knew about the dope and the booze, and the hedonistic sex. It was none of his business. They were all voters and he stayed in office by not pissing people off, but this was a murder and that's very different.

It had warmed up some and clouds had moved in from the west. Sheriff David J. Howes grew up in Hailey and knew the mountains well. He also knew by the clouds up north that it would be snowing up at Baker Creek and whatever evidence there might have been would be under new bright white soon and would be buried until May or early June at best.

"Well, thank you, everyone," He tipped his clean, white hat at John and Posey and walked out. His deputy was in the patrol car and they turned around in the middle of Main Street and headed north towards Baker Creek.

Chapter Forty-Five

Rupert and Rutter had a little meeting in the metal shop around the stove concerning Rowdey.

"He was a good lad," said Rupe. "I liked working with him. He was just at a stage where he should be raising a family, not chasing fast women in hot tubs."

"Maybe you're just jealous," said Jack.

"Why would I be jealous?" Rupe snapped back. "I've got a good wife at home, in my own bed. I don't need to be gallivanting around.

Sheriff Howes rolled up to the Payroll Office just in time for the morning meeting. The news of Rowdey's death rocked the little town of Triumph and it was on everyone's mind.

Swent stood at the door and welcomed the sheriff on in. His deputy stayed in the car and kept it running. It was very cold this morning, a storm had passed through and as always, the temperature plummeted afterwards.

"Hello, boys." Sheriff Howes knew Rup from the County Posse and Rodeo Club. They had ridden together on several occasions, searching for a lost child or a camper gone missing.

"We're dealing with a skilled sniper here, a pro. The gun was Russian made. The scope was a very good one. And the fact that the shooter tossed it in the snow and took off, makes me think it was a paid hit." His assessment took them all for a surprise. "Who would want to kill that kid?" he asked flatly.

"Nobody," said Rupe. "He was a good kid, never in trouble, this doesn't add up. The kid was crazy about this girl he had met, Anna, or Annie. She worked at the Lodge."

"I talked with her and she said that people got pretty crazy out at Gruner's."

"What kind of crazy?" Jack jumped in.

"Well," said the sheriff with a little bit of embarrassment, "seems some of them engaged in a large group sex event, kinda sounded like a snake ball ya might see down in the lava fields in spring."

"I knew it," said Jack. "That German was trouble."

"Miss Thatcher said that the German gentleman had offered to buy the victim's hat and was wearing it at the time of the shooting." The sheriff finally thought he was getting somewhere.

"The German was with the Harriman group that came out to see the mine a few days ago," said Jack. "He took chemicals from the mill and tunnels that could, under the right conditions, produce the snake ball you described. I knew it! The shot was meant for him, not the kid."

The Sheriff gave Rupe a look of agreed understanding and folded his note pad.

"I've got to find Mr Harriman. Guess I'll be headed up to the Lodge. Thanks, boys." And with that, he left.

Chapter Forty-Six

The production levels for the first quarter of 1939 were the best ever, "the Strike" was the reason, but the flood would slow things down some and the company needed to find more veins like the one they were working.

There were plans for a new mill of a new design.

"We are going to have a team of federal geologists in the hill this spring," Swent informed Rupe and Jack at the morning meeting.

"What for, boss?" Rupe asked.

"We are getting more government investment capital, new machinery, a new tunnel that will drive from the village all the way back to the Triumph shaft." Ed was pleased to say. "We can finally stop using that elevator at the 700-foot level."

"I'm going to miss that," Rupe joked. "When will all this get done?"

"Next year," said Swent. "Maybe '41, but it will get done. We are getting federal funding for the upgrades, and a new highway up into town from the rail spur."

"Really," said Jack. "Who's gonna pay for that?"

"Roosevelt, I guess," said the big Swede. "I don't care who pays for it, with the royalties we pay, we should get a smooth road to drive here on. My truck is taken a beatin' coming out here."

Jack lived in Hailey, in a neat, little house he built for himself and his family. He made the ride every day in his sedan.

"We produced about 854 tons of concentrate last month, more than our previous record," said Swent.

Chapter Forty-Seven

The Pennsylvania Railroad freight wagon pulled into the Bayway plant in central New Jersey. Although the plant was the site of the worst industrial accident in the state history, it was still operating after numerous court battles and alleged scandals involving workers going mad and dying of poisoning due to exposure to lead.

The box cars had made their way from Utah to New Jersey on the Union Pacific. The lead inside was from all over the Rocky Mountain states, but it could be safely said that a respectable percentage came from the number two producer in the country: The Triumph Mine's North Star Strike.

The very, patriotic men working deep in the hill behind the Sun Valley Lodge, unbeknownst to them, were going to send goods to the enemy.

IG Farben and Standard Oil had used their political clout to pressure politicians to allow this absurd trade by contending that Germany held equally important Synthetic Rubber patents and if our US corporations wanted to use those proprietary processes to make rubber, they needed to trade with use for Tetraethylene lead.

Men, women, and children on both sides of the battle lines would be shoveled into huge burial trenches, but we couldn't possibly violate patent rules, which are, after all, the measure of a civilized society.

The lead was unloaded. It had been cast into ingots in Utah at the ASARCO Smelter. The corporation that was once completely controlled by Meyer Guggenheim, had been hijacked by the stockholders and Meyer was forced to sit back and watch from the sidelines.

A man named Warburg got control of the majority of the stock and was calling the shots. After the war it was discovered that his brother worked for the Nazi war machine

Irene duPont had written letters to health officials protesting Standard oil production of TEL, a substance that DuPont themselves had created, but nobody was listening. The aircraft industry needed high octane fuels to operate and Wall Street was pushing for profits they could make on both sides of the Atlantic.

Brown Brothers Harriman had been trading so long with IG Farben that they couldn't stop unless they were forced to. Averell was part of the US War Department's political machine, but his hands were tied until Congress acted.

Congress was taking a hands-off stance on Europe's war. There were more Germans in America than any other ethnic group and Germany's move into Eastern Europe was none of our business. Nobody knew what was happening to the Jews and those that suspected were ignored. The lead was inloaded and put into the Ether Corps production line.

At about the same time, corporate executives at Hapaq-Lloyd's office in New York began to plan on an organized seizure of their shipping assets. They learned the hard way in World War I that freight ships delivering war supplies get sunk when war breaks out. The world's largest shipper lost their entire fleet in WWI and they did not want that to happen again.

They began pushing the US government to seize their ships, knowing full well that Germany would not stop at Czechoslovakia, but would go after the oilfields of Russia and North Africa, the latter being under the control of the Brits. If Hapaq-Lloyd didn't dock their ships in New York or Boston, they would end up at the bottom of the sea.

The situation in any major multinational corporation was the same in 1939. There were workers that were pro-Nazi and workers that were Jews and Italians.

Most of the big chemical cartels were German and within each corporate castle, there was intrigue and conflict.

Hapaq-Lloyd was the largest shipping company on the planet with ports in every major nation and agreements with numerous national, as well as, international organizations.

By August of 1939, Germany had prepared for war. Except for fuel to fly its dreaded Luftwaffe, the Fatherland had turned all of its plows into swords.

On a loading dock in Deepwater, New Jersey sat 500 tons of TEL, and twenty million dollars of aircraft fuel, made in America.

Chapter Forty-Seven

On August 29, 1939, the SS Bremen had unloaded it passengers at the #4 White Star dock in New York and that night was under tow moving across the Hudson Harbor to the Bayway dock of Esso.

There the liner was loaded with an explosive cargo of TEL, 500 tons, fresh from the kettles, twenty million dollars of aircraft fuel, in 55 gallon drums, and several hundred tons of phosphorus.

Just on the other side of Manhattan, at the 1939 World's Fair, a brochure in the General Motors Exhibit Hall read: *Our foreign trade has a stubborn vitality. How else could our export sales account for a 52% increase in the past five years.*

It had a stubborn vitality, alright. The Tetra Ethal Corp was like Miss Kitty selling bullets at a shoot out.

The SS Bremen was ordered to return to its Russian port of Murmansk. The ship was the pride of the Hapaq–Lloyd lines. It held the record for crossing the Atlantic at the blistering speed of 27 knots, almost 31 mph. That is flat-flying for a 1,000 foot ship.

On August 30, with nobody except her crew of 960 men, many loyal to Adolph Hitler, the super ship SS Breman pulled out past the Statue of Liberty, loaded with the goods that would drive the Nazi war machine. The crew began to paint her at sea a gray camouflage.

On September 1, 1939, Germany declared war on Poland as the SS Bremen headed back to the Russian port.

A few months later, she was set afire buy a disgruntled shipman. Her American cargo had been offloaded and delivered to the German military and this gave the German Air Force enough high-octane fuel to operate for the first year of the war and enough TEL to add to their existing fuel stocks for the following year. After that, they would be on their own.

Chapter Forty-Eight

In the spring of 1940, Wes, Rowdey's work partner, walked into the US Navy recruiter's office in Twin Falls, Idaho and enlisted.

"Well, are they going to take you?" asked Rupe. Both he and Rutter were very proud of the kid and wished him nothing but the best.

They never saw Annie again. She married and lived out her years in Connecticut.

Averell Harriman's banking assets were seized in 1944 and held until 1951 by the US government. In 1955, he became Governor of New York and the following year, he sought the nomination for President of the United States, but was defeated by Adlai Stevenson.

Chapter Forty-Nine

"I like your idea," Posey was staring off through her painting. She saw all the faces of her past in her mural and glad she had it to fall back on.

"What idea?" said Margaux.

"Your idea of taking off the year and skiing. Life's too short. You need to enjoy it while you can, because it ends before you know it." Posey was looking right through her soul.

"Did anybody get a weather report," I said.

"Snow, for the next four days. It's going to be a big one. You want another?" The old bartender took the empty beer bottle off the bar.

"No, thanks," I said.

"You ever been to the hot springs?" Margaux asked.

"No," I said.

"You got a 4-wheel drive?" She had a great smile.

"Yep. Brand new." I was already a month late on my payment to GMAC.

She grabbed her book bag and headed for the door. I followed. Posey lit another cigarette, "John," she said, moving her crystal glass ever so slightly.

"You know, you need to cut back." He was preaching to the choir.

She nursed another. John made it weak and she didn't complain.

As she gazed into her painting, the characters seemed to be moving, almost coming alive. She saw many of the men from her past. "It goes by fast, doesn't it, John?"

John just nodded and worked his bar, wiping a glass clean and placing it up on his back bar, right below his favorite mural, as he looked up at it, as he often did, it seemed to come alive for him too.

"Yea, it goes fast, boss."

www.ingramcontent.com/pod-product-compliance
Lightning Source LLC
Chambersburg PA
CBHW070539100726
47907CB00004B/1182